Sitting Ducks

Lisa Blower

 Fair Acre Press

First published 2016 by Fair Acre Press

ISBN 978-1-911048-01-5

Copyright © Lisa Blower 2016

The right of Lisa Blower to be identified as the author of this work has been asserted by her in accordance with the Copyright, Designs and Patents Act 1988.

a CIP catalogue record for this book is available from the British Library

Printed and bound in Great Britain by CPI Group (UK) Ltd, Croydon CR0 4YY

Design of Egg and Knockout pages: Tim Keates

Visit www. ...to read more about our books and to buy them. You will al... ...t-shirts, projects, competitions, news of author ...and may sign up for our newsletter.

For my Mum and Dad.

For pretty much everything really.

In front, on a little hill in the vast valley was spread out the Indian-red architecture of Bursley - tall chimneys and rounded ovens, schools, the new scarlet market, the crimson chapels, and rows of little red houses with amber chimney pots, and the gold angel of the Town Hall topping the whole... The sedate reddish browns and reds of the composition, all netted in flowing scarves of smoke, harmonised exquisitely with the chill blues of the chequered sky. Beauty was achieved, and none saw it.

Arnold Bennett, Clayhanger, 1910

The Conservative government pledges to take everyone with us, the frail, the elderly, the vulnerable, the poorest – we know they need protection.

David Cameron, 2010

Wednesday 5th May 2010

Round 1

Meagre in build. Mouthy in nature. One good owner and pottery trained: Josiah "Totty" Minton is bang out of sick notes and harbouring a dream of a three-bed semi with bay windows, fully-fitted carpets and enough of a garden to stretch his legs. He's had this dream for awhile though there have been other dreams. Simple ones. Pipe ones. Filthy ones. None of them ever come true. It's why he's so pissed off. Why he misses the urinal and pisses all over the floor.

He can't help it. Like they'll say they can't help him. And so he takes his piss and checks the time and finds he's ten minutes too early for his 10 o'clock appointment with the Jobcentre Plus in this arse-end of Stoke: a broad-bricked, flat-footed abscess, part glum concrete, mostly smutty glass, and home to the job-dodging and the feckless, the socially-needy and plain unlucky. It'd been another big idea from a man with no idea and built on a land that'd once been the pride of every dinner-table and the reddest on earth.

For this had been the Potteries. A once belching, smoking, grimy fug of high production and by royal design. A place that made things, did things, had things going on. Dreams? They made plenty. Some even came true. Now? It's a sorry old place, so sullen and sad. Its once proud skyline of milk-bottle kilns and smouldering stacks given up to slurry and slag after Thatcher's merry money-men robbed from the poor and gave to the rich, shutdown the pots and sold off the pits and ordered its workers to get on their bikes and pedal faster, boy, go faster.

Today, it's a place of flack and frustration, of rough futures and rusting flipcharts: Totty, if he could read, being told as he heads for a desk:

And to please sit down.

"Here?" he asks. "You want us to sit and do this here?"

"Yes," she says. "I do."

She is Maggie Gifford. She's the same age as Totty (44), though she's four stone heavier and one foot taller. As for the rest of her, she keeps her hair long and poorly conditioned, wears pearls, sensible shoes. She has a BA in Communications and a three-bed semi that she drinks a lot of wine in. Then she fights with her son. His father, her husband, had long left them for a girl who'd barely blown out the candles on her eighteenth birthday cake, and so when not asleep Jason was patrolling the streets with his hood up dealing small amounts of skunk he hid up the drainpipes round the back of the house in cling-film; his average customer not even coming up to your chest.

He's always on her mind as he never thinks of her, but for now, Maggie Gifford sits in her allocated carpeted paddock in a swivel chair in an office too hot with windows that won't open in front of a computer that takes ten minutes to boot up. To her left sits Richard, the last to kiss her stretch marks, the first to admit it was one big fucking mistake. To her right is Ruth, ever-so-sunny Ruth whom Maggie cannot stand. On her desk, Maggie keeps a pot of lidless biros, a mug of stone cold tea, and there's pills in her drawer far from herbal, extra strong mints and electronic fags. She looks across at Totty, who rubs at his jaw with a hand not quite withered but then not quite formed, and wonders what the hell to do with him.

Her computer screen tells her that he'd been first employed by Minton's from the age of sixteen. That he was laid off in 1986 and taken on by Sadlers until redundancy in early 2000. Then what? Sickness benefit 2001 - 2003. Long-term sick 2004 - 2007. Declared fit to work in 2009. In what, she did not know.

"Remind me Joshua," she says stiffly. "What have you been doing for work?"

"Joshua, Joshua, Joshua." It sounds so middling-class in his head. "I'm already the shit on your shoe without you getting my name wrong so let's get one thing straight. My name is Josiah. As in Wedgewood and Spode, as in man and brother." And she can tell by the look on his face that he is hoping to God she won't ask him to spell it.

She mutters a brief apology then turns to the computer for help. Sees his benefits were stopped three months ago but there was still no evidence of work. She asks, "Have you not been working at all?"

Totty looks down at the floor and sees paperclips (3), elastic bands (2), a mangy tissue and biscuit crumbs. "I look after my mother," he tells her. "She's terminally pig-sick."

There is a sigh from Maggie and a smile from Totty. She wonders if he was born with that hand not quite withered but then not quite formed, what the kids used to say at school, and she checks on the computer for disability allowance, claims she is sure he has made. Totty wonders for who cleans this place, if he had the right tools on him in his box right there to fix their Hoover, sort out that far wall with its chipped paint and damp patches, and then fleetingly thinks of his kids. Joss first. Kirty second. If they know he's been packing their rucksacks again for a move they won't want to do.

Maggie clips his thoughts and asks, "What about courses Mr Minton? Interviews? CV clinics? Did you ever finish an NVQ?"

Totty shakes his head at her questions. "No-one computerises these hands," he says, holding them up and waving. "They're skilled. They've grafted. They're what we've forgotten how to use."

"The thing is, Mr Minton, what concerns us here now..."

"I know a blue lady who ruined our lives. She championed plastic and charged us to buy. I know a blue lady who ruined our lives. And then she died."

Maggie ignores the song, his political ditty, if that's what it is, and opts for, "Mr Minton, you're not listening."

"No. You're not listening to me," and he points at the wall behind him. "What does that say?" He's gesturing towards the large Staffordshire knot that hangs from chains, its left side lower than its right, a plaque tacked on beneath it.

"What does what say?" Maggie lifts herself from the chair to look.

"That," he repeats. "I know you see it."

"You mean Industry and Prudence conquer?"

"Yes I mean industry and prudence conquer. Do you agree?"

Maggie chews on the side of her mouth and thinks about defrosting a couple of lamb chops for tea.

"Then what about that?" He's pointing again. This time with his left hand and this time she can see quite clearly that he's manacled to what looks like a toolbox with some sort of dog leash. Its contents sound heavy - he's lifting up the toolbox to show her, he wants her to take a good look - but Maggie is looking at the wall, at the coat of arms for Stoke-on-Trent.

She quotes. "It says, *vis unita fortior.* I don't know what it means. I don't know Latin."

"It means united strength is stronger," Totty tells her. "That we're all in this together."

He bangs the toolbox down on Maggie's desk. She jumps. He grins. His fingernails, she sees, are gnawed and dark with dirt and he was mildly good-looking once, she thinks, as he flicks up the catches and peers inside, she's seen him somewhere before; perhaps in here, maybe somewhere else. He roots noisily in the box before pulling out a spanner, holding it up to the light in admiration, deciding against it: it's not the weapon he needs right now. He will save that for later. He tells her, "We used to make all the crockery in the kingdom," running his fingers along a chisel's spine. "Now we can't grow a bloody teapot for toffee." And in his right hand is a claw-hammer. Not a large one and certainly not a new one, but still, it'll do the job and it's apt, being his father's an' all, and he tightens his grip around its neck and looks at Maggie from under his eyebrows.

"Don't tell me you've never dreamt of doing this yourself," he says, as Maggie emits, from between the fingers she's clamped over her mouth, some sort of squeal, a bleat of panic, of fear, that he might well strike her. She pushes her chair away from her desk and gets up.

"Mr Minton..." she begins, but he doesn't want to know.

He asks, "Do you have any idea of how many of us are out there just dying for something to do?"

She nods. She does. She knows better than anyone. Like she knows how Richard fixes the figures, does the maths, how he can't add up for shit. How those miscalculations make them look good at this Jobcentre Plus in this arse-end of Stoke, and they like to look good because they *have* to look good, because that's what keeps them in work.

"Mr Minton..." Maggie tries again, and this time she adds a please.

But he's not listening. If she can't hear him then he can't hear her and he shakes the toolbox to tease her. "Don't that sound good?" and she nods in case it helps and it's the right answer, as it's right under her nose now, the toolbox, and he's asking her to choose. "You can either put me out of my misery with this hammer to my head or you can choose solidarity and we can go kick fuck out of that wall." He shakes the toolbox again and, this time, screams in her face. "Matter!" he yells. "Fucking matter! Do it! Do it with me! We're all in this together!"

She chooses a long-handled screwdriver. Not because it's a choice, but because it's pot luck what she picks up first. She's crying and she wishes she wasn't because she's not a girl anymore, and she sniffs and she whimpers as he holds up his claw-hammer and makes to bring it down.

It was at that point that Maggie Gifford went hysterical. She battered hell out of the wall with that long-handed screwdriver until its end blunted and its rubber-grip flew off. And then she went at Richard with her bare hands. Fists actually. She punched the living daylights out of him whilst Totty, pinned to the floor by a security guard he was sure was in the class below him at school, laughed his fucking head off.

"Don't blame me," he told the paperclips and elastic bands, the mangy tissue, and the crumbs. "Blame the blue lady in her fine shoes and pearls. Who'd got so many men on her plate she didn't know what to do. So she had them working for broth without any bread then whipped their jobs from under them and put us all to fucking bed."

Round 2

Constance Minton pulled off a glove and rapped on the door. She wasn't expected but she wouldn't be a complete surprise either. News travelled quickly round this neck of the woods and she hoped that the man she was calling upon would be as sensitive to her situation as he'd been the last time she'd called upon him for his help.

She knocked a second time, then a third. This time the door swung open. A man with but an inch and a half on her in height, a good foot or so in girth, choppy boot polish hair and the glow of a woman finally proposed to, greeted her with a couple of headshakes, a deep sigh, and even a stifled laugh. She was no surprise if not later than expected and she was definitely pushing her luck.

He stepped aside so as to let the old woman in. Constance wiped her feet then removed her shoes, untied her headscarf and unbuttoned her coat. She hung everything up on coat-hooks and followed the man down a hallway and into his office where he directed her to sit in a mushroom leather rocker that looked and felt its price. She was yet to speak. So was he.

He was Malcolm Gandy, the head honcho of a private property enterprise that bought and sold on houses, trafficking tenants in between. He had many business cards in his back pocket – Director of Housing Services, Chief Housing Operator, Executive in Chief of Housing Operations, and, his particular favourite, Chief Executive Controller, Housing Division – as he traded under a variety of company names that he wore like days of the week underpants – MG Homes Plc, Gandy House & Home Ltd., Gandy & Gandy, Malcolm Gandy Estates.

How he acquired his properties was an equally sketchy business. He was known to have deals in place with nurses. He visited the old and the really very sick; had a weekly catch up with the council; and rumour had it there was a butterfingered copper who lost the odd file on a man sent down. But mainly he repossessed, from the living, from the dead, often swooping before the body had gone cold. There was never a brick left unturned or a deal not made and just to ensure he was never far away from scratching at a lacklustre pulse, he lived amongst his tenants, slap-bang in the rut, cock of all he surveyed, and with a ringside view of how folk kept his houses in trim.

Today, Malcolm Gandy was jam-packed into bespoke navy tailoring that pinched the skin under his armpits. His shoes shone. His eyes glinted. His fingers tapped on the desk. Neither he nor Constance wished to speak first.

Constance was no stranger to the place though she much preferred it in its former life, when it'd been Gandy's mother's house. A ratty mid-terrace with windows no bigger than thumbnails, Elsa Gandy had been left it by a gravel-voiced spinster aunt and had occupied it alone for the last two years of her life; the unfortunate timing of slowly-blinding cataracts meaning she never saw what she'd finally come to call her own. It'd broken Gandy's heart to watch her fumbling about its rooms, blind to the beauty of ownership.

"Mother," he had whispered, as she'd struggled to make him tea. "This is what *you* possess," and Elsa would wave him away with a flick of the sugar spoon and tell him that in her world, people were what mattered, not possessions.

"I don't know what you think you're doing putting me in here all on my own," Elsa had moaned, her fingers scarred with the cuts, splices, and splinters of a woman finding her way. "I was perfectly fine where I was. I knew that place like the back of my hand."

"But it wasn't yours mother," Gandy had insisted. "It belonged to somebody else."

"Of course it was *mine*," Elsa had retorted. "And then like every other house in this world, it becomes someone else's. You *pass on* Malcolm, not stockpile like you do," and she'd scuttled away from him, her stubbed fingertips caressing the walls as she had felt her way back to her chair.

Constance and Elsa had not liked each other, the pair of them renowned for their bickering and backbiting and yet most likely to be seen linking arms as they hopped from one pot bank to the next when worn down foremen could stand their squabbles no longer. And yet in Elsa's last months, Constance had become her most regular visitor. Not out of concern, but because at their age they couldn't afford to be picky about mates. They'd found that they'd still got a little stuff in common: they'd both had husbands not lovers, took two sugars in their tea. Both enjoyed crosswords, cleaning, and Countdown, and both had been raised in the two-up two-down terraces that had once housed potters and miners, tilers and steel-workers, brothers and sisters all piled in one room; a case of sleeping where you fell, eating what you were given, you turned up your wages on a Friday and your mother went up the bingo with it. Because family kept you alive in those days, both would agree. Not science and aspirin.

"You've got to listen to a house," Elsa had once told her son Malcolm, still unsure why he'd forced her to give up her home for a house she was lost in. "It'll soon tell you when it's tired of its contents."

But Constance had known alright. "It's not *your* house to rent out Malcolm. It belongs to the state."

"I don't know what you're talking about, Connie," Gandy, then twenty years younger, had replied.

"Yes you do," Constance had insisted. "Move Elsa out, lure some poor bugger in and charge double what the council would. It's daylight swindling, Malcolm. My tongue could run away with me. You could go to jail."

"And like I said," Gandy had replied with his competent grin. "I've no idea what you're talking about."

Gandy now studied Constance from behind his desk. Here she was again, ill and old and pretending to be neither with something to say that she wouldn't say; that even if he promised to do what she was really here to ask, she'd never just come out with it. He knew that's why she'd dressed smart for the occasion, had powdered her face, was wearing rouge.

"Connie," he said. "This has got to stop," and though Constance replied, "It will, it will," Gandy was unconvinced.

"Let's not forget, Malcolm, you'd be in jail if it wasn't for me and Totty."

Gandy yawned. It was a boring business. "I owe him nothing," he told her. "And it was thirty-two years ago Connie. No-one else saw what Totty thinks he did."

"But you sold the family-silver and then the bloody family," and Constance folded her arms and re-crossed her legs. "You owe us Malcolm Gandy. You owe *me*."

"Don't be nauseating," Gandy replied. "We all started out the same way. Pits, pots, we've all had the same chances."

"And we were all told that if you couldn't afford it you shouldn't have it."

"If we all followed that ethos Connie, this country would be on its arse."

"But loans buy greed Malcolm, and it's because of your bloody greed that most of us round here *are* on our arse."

"Come on Connie," he said. "There's no law on how many houses you can own."

"Well there bloody should be," she retorted. "No-one needs this much money, Malcolm, and no-one can possibly live in that many houses. You can't take a ruck of bricks with you and shrouds don't come with purses."

"I bought them fair and square," he shouted, holding up three fingers to emphasise his impatience. "Three months you've been in there, Connie. Three months."

And he was right. For the past three months, Constance and her family had been squatting opposite what had become known as the

Derelict Mile, land owned by a bankrupt subsidiary of Malcolm Gandy Estates. Why? Well, go back five years, and Malcolm Gandy Residential Ltd had bought four little terraces all in row on Bennett Road; houses so rundown and ramshackle that they'd only be worth anything if he knocked them down and started again. So he did.

However, he apparently ran out of money just before his diggers knocked on the door of No. 10. Dereliction, Gandy told the council surveyor investigating the Bennett Road demolition, was a costly business. Perhaps more costly than building completely new. He would go under if he demolished any further.

And so the residents on the other side of Bennett Road were forced to look out to a partly-boarded not quite flattened row of houses until eventually, numbers 1 to 13 were acquired by some other holding company with sly links to MG Homes.

Gandy reminded Constance yet again of the situation. "You've had plenty of notice Connie. Five years notice in fact, and plenty of options too." But Constance was busying herself with a long brown envelope wearing the council's logo, Housing Services, first class stamp.

"There's always an enemy within," she said, pushing the envelope towards him. It contained yet another final notice on the winding up of their tenancy agreement at 13 Bennett Road. "Though why you think you've got to own everything round here is quite beyond me. You're like a spoilt child." She pointed at the unopened letter. "Joss has his mocks at Christmas. He and Kirty walk to school together. They have friends, friends that'll stop remembering them. Then there'll be bus fares, early mornings, dark nights, and me; stuck in some old folk's bungalow up Smallthorne. I don't know anyone up Smallthorne, Malcolm, and what if there's no bus stop?"

Gandy sighed heavily. "Joss will walk his exams with his eyes closed," he began. "I've offered to pay for taxis to school for Kirty and Smallthorne, Connie, is not the end of the world."

"Then there's this business of social services snooping," Constance pressed on. "I mean we all know Lux. Never a motive always a whim, but now she's just being bloody nasty."

"I've no interest in gossip, Connie," Gandy interrupted. "I leave that to the amusement of you women."

Constance sneered. A perpetual muck-spreader, able to dredge up more dirt from under a fingernail than anyone else Constance knew, Lux Faithful (oh the irony!), being Joss and Kirty's mother, had lost custody of them three years back and yet continued to needle social services to investigate how they slept at night. In Lux's words: "My son's fifteen, my daughter has just turned seven, and they should not be sleeping on camp-beds in the middle of the front fucking room."

"Please don't do this," Constance asked Gandy. "You have all the other houses. Every single one of them. You don't need ours. Not really. Not yet. What would your father say if he knew what you were doing to us?"

Gandy glared. "You know better than anyone that I *never* looked up to that shit excuse for a man." He got up from his chair and sent it careering across the room. "He did nothing but hold me back. 'Don't get ahead of yourself son. Remember who you are'." He made a puking sound. "He was fucking nothing and he gave me even less. They'd still be sitting on the street with their suitcases if it wasn't for me. "

"And if it wasn't for us, Malcolm, you'd have nothing to show for it either," Constance sniffed. "You'll never be better than us, however much you try to forget who you were. But if you've an ounce of decency left, you'll stop all these letters, tell Lux to go home, and give my Totty some regular work." She paused. Looked down at her hands. "He needs to work Malcolm, you know he needs to work. He needs to think he's still got a side to fight on."

"You know exactly what he needs to do," Gandy reminded her. "Because where is he Connie? Why isn't *he* here? Where is he right now?"

"Then wait," Constance demanded, biting her lip. "For the sake of Joss and Kirty. It's my right to die in the house that I was born in."

Gandy rolled his eyes. "Connie," he said flatly. "You're squatting in my property and I want my property back. I know you mean well but the deadline is still next Friday. You've both been offered good homes. Don't prolong this out of principle. It wasn't paradise then. It was a fucking dirt bowl."

She shook her head defiantly. "Then you really will have my death on your hands. And you will Malcolm. I'll make sure it's seen as all your fault," and with her hand clamped over her runaway-mouth for effect, she turned and fled his office knowing that it'd been a battle well-staged and fought.

Round 3

Looking backwards was now a way of life for Police Constable Frank Blatch. With his strong chin, dull eyes, and whiff of quiet tragedy, he'd been dealt a batch of life's slim-pickings, in looks, in family, in lady-joy, but had somehow impressed Her Majesty's constabulary since leaving college, remaining in the same job for near on twenty years with no desire to move up, go sideways, or jump ship. He had his car. He had his regular patrol. He monitored passing traffic with a speed camera. He sometimes tracked joy-riders and had his eye on a car-ring. But mainly it was surveillance, watching and waiting and jotting down notes. Right now, he was midway through compiling yet another report that wouldn't see the light of the day, since campaigning for a series of speed bumps along a stretch of road renowned for its reckless drivers who never looked left, was not high up on traffic agendas.

Occasionally, his superior would dangle him a carrot but he'd wave it away. He'd lost his wife Sissy to a hit and run five years back and had been dedicated to slowing things down ever since. He never did get the big rush, not when everything was temporary, everyone just passing through, and though the one criminal he kept letting slip through his fingers was grief, Frank was generally considered too loyal to fire, too thorough to discipline, and so he was just left alone to do his rounds and file his reports; a spreadsheet whore who produced files so large it was a station joke that if Frank should ever throw the book, he would be done for murder.

It was, however, far easier for Frank to play paperwork than catch a thief. In fact, if he was honest, he'd probably not given a shit about his job since the ear-splitting screech of some botch-job brake pads had taken his wife's life at 16:02 on 9th May 2005. It's why he lived in his patrol car, the wells behind the seats strewn with landfill, and where he'd sit, night after night, going over his last words to Sissy before she'd stormed out to buy milk.

"You don't ever forget *her* bloody shopping," Sissy had started the argument. "I bet Constance Minton's got milk coming out of her ears."

Constance Minton. She had been more of a mother to Frank than his own ever was. She'd nursed him through the measles, mumps, and whooping cough after his own mother had told him not to fuss, blow your nose, and take a pill. She'd talked him out of using those blunt-looking scissors when, lumbering about as a pockmarked teenager, big as a hummock and petrified of the opposite sex, he'd locked himself in the bathroom to contemplate whether his impending adulthood was really for him. She'd ordered him to go get the girl before her train left, and then to get her down the aisle before she had the time to take off her coat. But it was also Constance who occupied many of his thoughts. "Because really Frankie," Constance would say, as she buttered his bruises and iced his black-eyes from the fights he didn't start. "You're the son I should've really had a hand in making."

And so Frank, coming home from work without the milk he'd promised to pick up, had apologised once more to Sissy. Useless wasn't the word. He'll pop out for the milk in a bit. Just don't keep on.

"You know I've got to see her right," he'd told his wife. "Life's not been kind to Connie, and I'm really all she's got."

"It's not always kind to me either!" Sissy had shouted back. "She has her own son Frank and you are my husband. A husband who promised me Spain. 'You and me, Sissy,' you said. 'We'll go and live the life of bloody Riley on the Med.' Well, we're still here. And you promised me four pints of milk."

"He's got no work!" and even Frank had been surprised for how loud he'd shouted this at his wife. "They'd be on the streets if it wasn't for me. I won't see Connie or those kiddies without food on the table or a roof over their heads. It's family Sissy. I know you don't get it but to me, it's family."

Sissy had stood over him. Hands slapped on big hips. Her stodgy face reddening with being ever so very cross at knowing her husband was paying the Minton's monthly rent. "You know what I think Frank

Blatch?" she'd said. "I think you chose me because I was as near to Constance Minton as you could possibly get. Why else would you take a second look at someone like me?"

Her expression now haunts him. He's long been afraid of the truth in her words. He wishes every day that he'd answered her, prolonged the argument, and not, as he had, neglected to respond.

Because his silence had made her mad and because she was mad she'd gone to get the milk herself. And if he hadn't forgotten to pick up four pints of milk as she'd asked, Sissy would still be here, hands slapped on hips, that stodgy face of hers breaking into a smile as she set about making him a rice pudding so voluptuous, he could only assume she'd made it in heaven.

*

Frank was now marching Totty across the park, towards a grassy knoll that they'd often played on as kids - bows and arrows, their fathers' screwdrivers for pistols - *Pow! Pow! You're dead!* - Frank pushed Totty to the ground, pulled back his left leg and kicked him in the back. It wasn't his best left boot, a tap with the heel at best: he'd been no footballer, crap at sports, never could kick a bo' against a wo and 'ed it til it bost. But it still made Totty wince and curl up into a ball. Frank kicked him again. Then again. Kicked the toolbox in the end. There were only so many blows a man already down could take.

"I had to do something to find you," Totty tried to explain. "We were having a conversation Frank. A conversation we never finished."

"So you threatened Maggie Gifford in broad fucking daylight with a hammer?" and Frank was hopeless with rage. "You're just bloody lucky I was round the corner and got to you first."

"Well where the fuck have you been?"

"Out."

Which wasn't entirely untrue because Frank had been out. A lot. In his car. Watching the traffic. Surveying the scene. Watch long enough and something will come to light. There had to be other reasons why Sissy had died on that particular stretch of road near the precinct. A pothole maybe. Cracked tarmac. Blind corner. Blazing sun. Something had distracted the driver who'd hit her and driven off. The zebra-crossing Sissy would have been using was as bold as the brass Frank sometimes picked up just to chat with, to fill up those lonely early hours when Sissy's face was at its clearest, her voice at its strongest. "You promised me Spain Frank. You promised me four pints of milk."

Frank suppressed the urge to kick Totty again. He often wondered how to be the law with a law unto himself; why it was that he saved him every time. He had an inkling that perhaps Totty's dole had been stopped. Another new legislation had been passed, more whimpering about public cuts reducing national debt: it'd taken one government to set up the welfare system, all others to dismantle it as they worked out the cost. *The money has to come from somewhere*, as they kept on saying, and not everybody thought it a fair spend.

But blokes like Totty, they relied upon it. It was a weekly wage when there was no wage. When the jobs he didn't know about, didn't qualify or scrub up for left him broken, in crisis, in bits. When he was last in first out, or taken aside by the gaffer who'd thought that his withered left hand must have the light-fingers, butterfingers; when those gumball eyes, that could barely read a word, seemed to understand every entitlement on the contract verbatim. Men like Totty Minton weren't ideal candidates. *Sorry lad. Not this time. Times are hard.* Men like Totty Minton were everywhere and nowhere and now, more than ever.

And yet he still took the jabs in the guts, stuck on a plaster and got up, looking for more. Call it stamina. Call it belligerence. Call it breezeblocks of self-belief. Frank would see Totty drudging about the estate as he patrolled by in his car. Wind down the window, offer him a fag. *What's to do, comrade?* Painting and decorating lad. *Tomorrow?* Plasterer wants a right hand. *The day after that?* One thing leads to another, comrade. I'm a man about town.

"You don't know what it's like Frank, big man like you in a uniform with a purpose," Constance would say when Frank popped round with their rent money. "He's had the stuffing knocked out of him time and time again, and you know what they say. You either look after or you're looked after and once you're being looked after and you know you'll get looked after, then that's the end of it." Because everyone knew that was the other thing that welfare could do. And that Totty simply didn't tick enough boxes.

Frank looked down at the heap of old overalls on the grass. He caught sight of the aggravated stare. Totty did not exactly encourage respect and Frank asked him yet again, "What is it that you want?"

"You know what I want," and Totty was going to have to say it again. "You've got a house sat at home you won't fucking live in!"

"I've a house that is *mine* comrade. Bought. Paid for. *Mine*."

"You're not fucking living in it!"

"It's *my* house!"

"They're going to take my kids Frank. You know they will and I can't lose them. I fought tooth and bloody nail for them in court. Those kids are all I have."

At this, Totty chucked a dog-eared Polaroid of a crumpled brother and sister sat on the swings up Hanley park at Frank's feet. "I need to get them out of here Frankie. What the fuck do you expect me to do?"

Frank picked up the photograph. It was one he'd not seen before but it was one he remembered taking. *"Now Frank! Take it now! Look how high I am! Look at me!"* Kirty's legs just skirting his head in those dungarees she'd cajoled him into buying. "Everyone has a pair Frank," a picture in a catalogue. "Everyone but me." £15.99 and a smile that had broken his heart. Little Kirty Minton with her gumball eyes and sheet of the blondest hair reminded him that there were still bits of joy to be had in the world. "You're the best, Uncle Frank," her arms tight around his neck. "Can you be my dad too?"

Frank kicked at the toolbox again. "You idiot," he spat at Totty. "Wielding a hammer in the Jobcentre and at Maggie fucking Gifford? Are you right in the head? She wants to press charges. She thinks there's compensation in it. She says you threatened her life."

"I was desperate!" and Totty threw his hands up in the air. "How was I to know she was a fucking head-case with a drink problem?" but he met with Frank's fist and he was back on the grass again nursing his temple.

"I should throw away the key and let you rot," Frank shouted. "The answer is no Totty. No. No. *No.*"

Totty started to laugh. "My old man always said that pride makes everyone cling onto the living room furniture, but take a look upstairs and you'll see just how poor they are." He spat onto the grass. "Yet who sits on your settee Frank? Who actually sits on your fucking three-piece and lives when everything's dead upstairs?"

Frank ignored him and kicked the toolbox again. Totty's scruffy politics were not something he entertained anymore and he wasn't about to start giving them the time of day now. Still, he had to ask, "Where d'yer get the wedge to pay for all of this?"

"All part of the crusade and tools of the trade," Totty grinned, rubbing at his mouth and finding blood. "Long live society eh Frank?" bloodied spittle on the grass. "Long live this fucking beautiful workless society and all the fields we churn up for new homes."

Frank rolled his eyes and turned away. He'd had enough now. Seen enough. Enough, he thought. *Enough.*

"That'd be right old friend," Totty called after him as Frank lit a fag and began to stroll away. "Pull the plug on the sink and put the rest of the world out of our price range. Isn't that what you homeowners call a fucking democracy?"

But Frank was already back in his car and driving away.

Round 4

Kirty Minton's hand shot straight up as soon as her teacher Miss Knight asked if there were any other questions, preferably sensible ones, for despite having the appeal of bellybutton fluff, Councillor Dingwall had sportingly endured –

"What car do you have?"

"What trainers do you wear?"

"What would you sing on X-Factor?"

"KFC or McDonalds?" And,

"Can you give Stoke City more money to buy new players?"

Miss Della Knight, newly-qualified and seven months pregnant with a brain like fudge, was functioning on very little sleep and anything on toast; her old single bed in the back bedroom of her childhood home proving far too slender for her growing frame. She'd split from the father after six years of make-do love, the icing on this bun in the oven being that he didn't want to be a father when he was a social worker working for children and families: "With a job like I have, Della, you've got to focus on the kids whose parents don't give a shit outside of the benefits they get for them. Don't you see? Being a father will make me a father to them all and I can't father them Della. I have to walk away."

And so that's what she'd done instead. It was a fact, she'd yelled. Not a reason. And if he didn't want a baby then he didn't want a family. "Just those that you can close the door on at half five," she'd said. "But you'll get caught out Jake. One day, one of those kids will break your heart and you won't have a family of your own to come home to who can put you back together."

She'd turned up on her mother's doorstep with her luggage and fat ankles assuring her that she needed little more than a few weeks of breathing space and some sleep.

However, her temporary board and lodgings, where the largest of her suitcases remained on the living room floor, since neither she nor her mother had been able to carry it up the stairs, was now the least of her worries. Sheena Liquorice, Headmistress at the school she was teaching at, had recently alerted her to clause 8.1 on her contract:

8.1. To qualify for School leave and benefits, a member of staff should have been continuously employed by the School for a minimum period of 12 months before the expected week of confinement/adoption.

"Rules are rules Della," she was told, Sheena being an out of scale brontosaurus of a woman with sallow skin and heavily-dyed hair, so far unimpressed with Miss Della Knight so good on paper with lovely handwriting. "And people like us don't make the rules. Besides, maybe some time out will do you good."

Because Della was a teacher too-concerned. And she was becoming far too-concerned for a girl called Kirty Minton.

"I still want to make a referral," Della had announced to Sheena, pushing the contract aside. "I know they're a family fluent in social services but I'm very concerned for her mental health. She told me to go stuff myself today because I was part of generation greedy-guts. I only asked if Kirty Minton could be in my class today and not the chef she was pretending to be. Generation greedy-guts Sheena! That's what she said to me. Doesn't it concern you that this situation has been allowed to fester like it has?" And so Sheena had spelled it out.

Referrals to social services meant problem pupils and since problem pupils disrupt classes and knock the school's average marks down, that would mean inspection; unscheduled drop-in's from Ofsted representatives. That meant paperwork. Reams and reams of it. And steering groups. Councillors. Extra money for teaching assistants and new computers with new fangled systems no-one would understand. A member of the family elective on the PTA would get wind. And because the school's funding is result-dependent, no headmistress worth her salt wanted to report in to her PTA that her team was failing, especially when a year off retirement. That would certainly affect contributions to the new mini-bus.

"But don't you care?" and Della had been beside herself with frustration. Sheena, on the other side of the desk, had remained nonplussed.

"Fundraising and masking tape is what keeps this school running, Della," she had said. "Jam tarts and jumble sales. Don't start boosting hopes that won't see the light of day. They've enough disappointment in their lives as it is," and she'd returned her attention to the letter she was drafting and reminded Della of the location of the door.

Della had been forced to return to her class where Councillor Roy Dingwall's PR trail was shifting into third gear. She nodded in Kirty's direction, "Yes Kirty, what would you like to ask the councillor?" and crossed her fingers behind her back. *Please don't make me look like I can't do this.*

"Mr President," Kirty began, her gumball eyes wide (her father's doing) and her hair so long it was a wonder it didn't rip when she sat down (her mother's doing). "Do you have any jobs going spare? It's just that I've really outgrown being a child."

Local Tory Councillor Roy Dingwall was, 24hours before the General Election, attempting to showcase his fluffier side to his constituents by sitting in a class of what he'd called "our exciting future." He'd earlier instructed the accompanying local TV cameras to film him from the right owing to shaving rash and flared glands, and he was slumped on an infant's plastic chair like fifteen tons of coal, an open and upside-down copy of *Stig of the Dump* on his lap; the suggestion being that he'd read aloud to these under-privileged youngsters, carefully selected by local television researchers for the ways in which they "survived" amidst mass unemployment, reckless parenting, and shanty-style bedrooms complete with Sky and X-Box.

A conniving bastard at the best of times, Councillor Dingwall was like many other politicians who'd been caught out spending their life from a borrowed purse. A sixty-something thick-set man with a heavy brow, heaving thighs, and a little gummy when he smiled, Roy had been desperate to win back fans after six months of excruciating headlines about his expense claims. He had since defected to the right, after a decade or two on the left, and was now re-pitching himself for parliamentary business as a blue. He had outspoken views on immigration - "We're renting our country from *them* now!" - and social housing - "You want a sea view? Then vote with a C because L is for lodger which means digs and not homes." Which is why his son, heading up his campaign trail, had suggested it'd be beautiful PR for him to spend the Wednesday before the election as a visible sympathetic force amongst the disadvantaged kids making the best of it in the sink.

Roy was, therefore, in a brutal mood by three o'clock that afternoon, keen for the oversized blue rosette on his lapel to get more screen time than the children, and preferably do all the talking. He gave a small cough, readying himself to finally answer the little girl who'd been patiently awaiting his reply.

"With ambition like that," his right hand balled into a fist, "we can safely say we have our new generation of iron ladies right here." And spying his opportunity to launch into policy, he spoke of the importance of "the kids" getting out there and volunteering in the name of Cameron's Big Society. He strongly emphasised the phrases, "Ambition should begin at home," "No-one can do it for you," and "It's *your* community," with a pointed finger at the camera; Kirty, by this point, background scenery.

"Yet the only way for these children to learn to stand on their own two feet is for the government to get the country back on its feet by producing again, manufacturing," Della interrupted. "This is not your average classroom of advantaged scholars, but twenty-seven kids whose futures are being shaped, right now, by all that the Tories dismantled pre-Blair, and then neglected to rebuild in favour of outsourcing cheaper labour abroad. I agree that ambition should begin at home, but you can't fuel ambition when there's no food on the table."

Roy coughed a second time and gestured for the TV cameras to stop rolling. Kirty's hand shot up in the air again and the cameraman swiftly adjusted the angle to refocus on the photogenic seven year old and her very determined face.

"I have ambition Mr President," Kirty assured him. "I practise being a different job every day. This morning I was a dentist so I took all the wisdom out of my Nan's teeth. She says that what she knows is all that's worth knowing round here."

At this, Roy gestured for the cameras to *keep* rolling and said with a beaming smile, "I'd like to meet your Nan young lady. We need more stalwart citizens like her."

"Why don't you tell her yourself?" Della blurted out. "I'm sure she would enjoy the conversation."

Roy launched himself out of the chair sending it clattering behind him. He opened his mouth to bellow his disdain as his son pointed out that, "Actually dad. It would be beautiful PR."

Round 5

"The animal kingdom has always swarmed with predators," said Ursula Rawson-Sage, middle manager for Children and Young People, Central Staffordshire Social Services, as she began to conduct Jake Povey's supervision, two hours behind schedule, in their local Costa Coffee. "I know you're vegetarian Povey, but don't let your heart rule your mouth on this one. You do your job, you go home then you ask yourself, if the boot was on the other foot, would they do the same for you?"

She was stood at the counter deliberating between muffin or teacake, skinny or soya, in much the same way that she was still mulling over whether to label herself wife or civil partner, and whether or not to put her hand on Jake's leg as she was prone to do when spouting her insight into how the other half lived. She was dressed head to toe in her traditional black, partly to shrink a dress-size, partly because it suited her bleak frame of mind, her bleached blond hair shorn and spiked and hardened with too much gel.

"It's just part and parcel of what we do," Ursula's supervision patter in full flow. "But don't start playing detective or make it into some personal beef you can't digest. Focus on the case in hand, not on the hand that feeds them."

"And it's all happened before and it'll all happen again," Jake replied, gesturing for the barista to double-up his espresso order whilst hunting for spare change in his trouser pockets. "Turkey, Greece, Tenerife. Where was Lux this time, Gibraltar? The sea is always bluer, the sun shines out of another waiter's arse. It's a total waste of time and money to start proceedings that just aren't needed. She'll be gone again in six months."

"And you're not yet a parent Povey. So how will you ever expect to know when a child needs their mother, when a father must man up into their father?"

Jake snatched up his espresso from the counter and gulped quickly. "Seriously Ursula," he said. "Grow up," and he dumped his empty espresso cup down on the counter, picked up his rucksack, and threw his jacket over his arm. Ursula caught hold of him.

"Don't be mardy. We're all knackered. We've all got too many kids to think about and are managed by insularity and bad practice. I warned you when you came into this job, it's grot per metre here. This sort of shit will make your eyes water. You'll think this is the road to Wigan Pier. But you've had three legitimate referrals on your desk for over six weeks now, Jake. The Mintons *are* a case. There is threshold. So sort it. And soon."

Jake looked down at the floor, his eyes flickering between ripped sugar sachets, tacky napkins, and sticky table legs. One of six social workers jostling for desk-space in the basement office of Care Management 3, Jake and the rest of the team were responsible for over one hundred children; more than half were looked after - foster care, adoption, sheltered housing, refuges - at least 35% were on the child protection register, and they were following up over eight new cases a week. In the office next door were the seven similarly knackered and ashen-faced employees manning the good-ship Care Management 4 with a similar long list for the same small patch and shooting up so much caffeine and cigarettes that the butt buckets were emptied twice a day, the toilets on a permanent flush.

It's why Jake couldn't understand why Ursula should be pushing the Mintons up the priority list when a case like them (no obvious neglect, abuse, depravity) should've been considered too low-level for their involvement. By now, a call would've been put in to one of the various agencies or charitable arms that stepped in when social workers stepped away, and the whole case wouldn't be given a second thought. And yet there was this impatient queue of referrals about the Mintons and Jake mulled them over in his mind:

(1) This was a formal correspondence from their mother via Goodlove Solicitors. Lux Faithful would poison the apple a couple of times a year and then file complaints when no-one took a bite. Her referrals were troublesome and malicious but never bore much weight given the marriage of her prolonged absences and profound selfishness; the

result of children bearing children and everyone growing up as mates. Not to mention her appointment of Derek Goodlove's shady law outfit that specialised in speculative compensation claims, preferably for whiplash or state harassment (his marketing featured the line - *"Social Workers Hammering at your Door?"*)

(2) This was a handwritten letter from Miss D. Knight, primary school teacher and Jake's ex, using the sort of labels that should stay in textbooks. She claimed to feel that she was *"an unwilling accomplice in the ignorance of a child at risk who uses fantasy to mask unhappiness and fear."* Jake had had to stop himself from tearing the letter to shreds.

(3) This was a series of emails from Heather in Housing, firing off her final notices and severe warnings between sun-bed appointments which, post-landing on the Minton doormat, were being used to line the cat litter tray.

"Come on Ursula," said Jake, steadying his temper. "Would you engage with Housing services trying to evict you if you were eighty-five and had lived there all your life? I just don't get what we're pursuing here?"

"The same that we always pursue," Ursula said, leading him towards an empty table. "Only what's right for the children," and she dumped down her bag, spilt coffee into her saucer, pulled out a pen from behind her left ear, and flopped down into the chair.

The Mintons had been known to social services since Totty's second redundancy in 2000. They'd first been a client of Ursula's - then newly-qualified and chomping at the bit - when five year old Joss Minton had been found alone chewing on fag-butts on the floor of a phone box. His father had been making a series of crank calls to his old boss having found out that directing the firm into administration warranted him a tax-free bonus of a hundred and fifty odd grand.

Totty had neither disguised his voice nor curbed his rage and had made a series of "nasty little threats" that had made his ex-boss feel "stressed out and scared for my life." The police deemed the episode a domestic but cautioned Totty nonetheless. Ursula had gone to the house and taken tea with Constance Minton who, at seventy-five then, was barely scratching the surface of old age. They had got on well, had quite a laugh actually, and by the end of the week the whole misunderstanding had been brushed under a new hearth rug from Stoke market.

Six months later, and Ursula had received a phone call from a woman called Lux Faithful. She was not dead, as Constance had previously insisted, but had been out of the country on business. She'd returned to 13 Bennett Road to find her son Joss home alone and feeding his school tie to the gas fire. Where was everyone else?

Totty was, at the time, being talked down from throwing himself off the top of the multi-storey car park by Police Constable Frank Blatch with a packet of Marlboro's and the woman whose car it was he'd chosen to use as a springboard.

Constance was, at the time, shouting for a full house up Hanley bingo pocketing a life-changing £200 which she spent on another new hearth rug, a chippy tea, and new shoes for the kids (Clarks). The rest she kept in a make-shift drawer in her bedside cabinet she thought no-one knew about, but which Totty regularly snaffled tenners from and never put back. Both had assumed that the other was looking after Joss. Both didn't rush home when called but waited for the next bus.

Since then, the file had gone from strength to strength and passed through social workers like running water. Three times Lux had fled the country "on business" and returned to make her standard malicious referrals when Constance refused to let her play house. Three times Lux and Totty had broken up then reunited, one particular reunion being long and fruitful enough to produce Kirty in 2003. And God only knows, thought Ursula, how many times Totty had been found at the top of the multi-storey threatening to chuck himself off if he had to spend another night in "that shit-hole piece of charity," presumably being another place allocated by social housing when social work investigations deemed 13 Bennett Road unsuitable for family life.

It was anti-depressants that made a Minton world go round, they joked in the office of Care Management 3, for there was neither love

nor money between a Minton, and what with Constance's apron-
strings still throttling her son, no social worker was ever truly able to
get to the man himself. Some said, *Totty Minton, does he even exist?*

"But there's something else a matter with you," Ursula muttered at
Jake. "You've lost your objectivity, got entrenched in the bullshit."

Jake looked down at his shoes in reply. He had not yet let on about
his split with Della and their imminent child.

"See," she said, pointing her finger at him. "You're evading me like
a client."

"No I'm not," he began. "I'm just not agreeing with you. I don't
think the Mintons *are* a case when the problem's going to be solved
as soon as they move out. Besides, they're ticking all the boxes.
They're clean. They're fed. They go to school. This cannot be about
two fucking camp-beds and your personal agenda."

"It's not," Ursula replied. "It's about what's right. And what *isn't*
right, Jake, is that we still have a fifteen year old boy sleeping aside
of a seven year old girl on two camp-beds in the front room' of a
council house they were evicted from three months ago," and she
paused to sip at her coffee as if blotting her lipstick.

"Twice they've been given other houses with separate bedrooms
and proper beds for the kids. Twice they've done a runner and turned
back up at Bennett Road. Twice we've had to fight compensation
claims for the trauma we apparently caused in… what was it now?
Unreasonable enforced relocation. I've lost count for how many get-out-
of-jail-free cards I've got dickhead-dad because he's lost his rag in
public. I can't remember how many courses I've enrolled him on, how
many grants I've got him that have paid him to learn to read. Youth
Offending have made it more than clear on how high-risk Joss is in
terms of his behaviour, but because it gets hidden in A grades and
everyone loves a pin-up from the sink, we um and we ah and we um
and we ah, until one day um and ah won't bring the lad back to life
because Joss Minton got mad because he thinks he stole his new
Nikes. And though I'm more than aware of Lux's perpetual jet-
setting, she *is* their mother Jake," and Ursula, clocking the time,
gulped down the rest of her coffee.

"What's that supposed to mean?" Jake snapped. "You're never on her side?"

"It's our job to be on the side of the children," she told him. "And it'll do you good to remember that when Constance Minton is wooing you with her Bakewell tart tomorrow, because that's what she does Jake. She controls and she suffocates and she's stealing their lives," and she tossed the file into Jake's lap. "Get it sorted Povey. You know I don't like missing targets and being made to look soft."

Jake added the file to the rest of his caseload, gave her a mock salute and left.

Round 6

Constance Minton stood in her front parlour window at 13 Bennett Road and looked out at what she could see of Derelict Mile.

No.2 had been the Arkinstalls. He was a drunk. She'd brawl in the street.

No.4 would fetch the police.

No.6 were the Baggerleys. Violet and Roger and the tallest of sons. He was always doing "ever so well, Connie. You should see the size of his new company car." But that was Violet. Big handbag and no draws and that smug you'd think her Aunty had come up from Brighton.

No.8 and Constance had to think. He went in a home, or he put her in a home. Either way, one of them lost their marbles and the house had to look after itself.

No.10 had been there almost as long as she had. Keithy Harries and Marge. Brother and sister, left to fend for themselves when their mother dropped dead of a heart defect back in the day when defects weren't found and illnesses had no fancy names.

No.12 faced their house. Winnie Wilson, as dull and cheerless as her window nets, and parked up on her doorstep with her woodbines telling anyone who'd listen that she'd been born in a poorhouse up Chell.

Constance missed them all and wished them all back, and she went into her kitchen and looked up at Ned's photograph. "You bugger for leaving me," she said, as she checked her four pork chops under the grill with her thumb. Decadence was not something she favoured, duck egg blue flaking and peeling off her kitchen walls even less so, and she lowered the flame and set about peeling a bag of spuds at the sink, muttering – "all that dust on his lungs, yet no-one sweeps enough off the streets."

Because Constance Minton told folk that her husband had died from a bronchial disease, his lungs like two full Hoover bags when they cut him open from half a century of pot bank graft, and not from a thick length of rope he'd tied tight about his neck up the woods. Sometimes, she even cried.

Constance's first reaction to the front doorbell was ignorance. No-one called at the front door except the council with their eviction notes, or the Jehovah's witnesses that she sometimes invited in for tea. *"Do you believe in family and hope?"* Of course she did! That's what she was fighting for. And they'd leave exhausted by her preaching. But then came the loud flick of the letterbox, a rat-a-tat-tat that Constance assumed to be the local rag. Eventually, she heard Kirty hollering. She dropped the potato peeler in the sink and rushed towards the front door.

She was greeted by her granddaughter and Roy Dingwall's bitter little smile. She clocked him straightaway as being that shameful politician who'd claimed the fitting of a gastric band on expenses during a second honeymoon in LA. He clocked her as the squatting Bennett road battleaxe who'd been refusing to budge on account of her human rights: *It's my God-given right to die in the house I was born in*. He offered his hand in the shade of the afternoon sun and asked her if she was keeping well.

"Well?" Constance replied. "It depends if I can afford to be."

Because she was no longer too clever on her legs these days and while her bones were thinning and the aches nagged on, cancer, she was sure of it, was finally rearing its head in a horse-chestnut sized lump in her left breast.

She was yet to tell a soul. Constance Minton wasn't interested in being ill and she'd no time to be dying yet either. She was make-do and mend and had already survived much. "And we all get sick and die, let's face it, we do," she'd tell her son Totty whilst grilling him a nice bit of gammon for his tea. "But you're not telling me that our souls don't work this hard in this life to not go on somewhere better. Why else would your father have done what he did to us?" And she'd cast a half-hearted glance up at Ned, hanging in a frame above the stove in a black and white world, the snap snapped up Rhyl, or was it on Llandudno pier, sometime in the early 60-s, the pair of them bickering over whose fault it was that she was almost forty and yet to bear a child.

Roy stood looking with bemusement at Constance's cluttered window box, its plastic flowers drooping and blazing like a damp Bonfire night."It's only ever about affordable housing Mrs Minton," he offered, amazed how realistic the ivy looked. "It really isn't personal at all."

"This *was* affordable," Constance snapped back. "It *was* affordable living. My house. Next door. This road. This estate. But you lot went and made it affordable housing for leeches like Gandy to buy so we can't afford to live."

Roy's mouth dropped open, as Kirty piped up to save his bacon. "Did you know that if your house is your home then your home is always your house?"

Roy smiled gratefully. "Goodness," he began. "That's quite some question."

"It's not a question," she told him. "It's a point. But if you're going to give me a job I'll forgive you," and she parted from his company to show off her very best cartwheels down the road.

"So, you see, I've ever so sorry duck," Constance said with a hint of snob. "But I'm just nipping out for a loaf." And she shouted for Kirty to come in and do her homework.

Della stepped forward and offered her hand. "You'll know that this is Councillor Roy Dingwall, Mrs Minton, and we're here because he visited Kirty's school today. This is local TV who are filming him, canvassing, and they'd like to film him having a cup of tea with you." She stopped. She sounded so stupid. She clamped her hands to her cheeks and shook her head. "It's shameless publicity, Mrs Minton," followed by a small laugh. "I don't really know why we're here at all, but whilst I'm here, would Mr Minton be at home at all? I'd really like to have a word."

Constance glared at Della. "Who are you?"

Roy assumed the question was for him. He said, "Mrs Minton, if you would accept my apologies for I know the reaction of my own wife when unannounced guests drop by with the expectation of tea, as you know better than anyone that community was dealt out with the ration bags. But in the name of a bigger and better society..."

"There is no society duck," Constance interrupted. "Not anymore and certainly not according to you lot. Weren't right, you said, that folk like us should cast our problems on *your* society. Yet you bloody Tories shut down every last bit of industry round here and killed our society. Can't be a society when there's no bloody jobs and I'll tell you this for nothing: it's no life on the dole, because have you ever seen a grown man take his own life because his self-worth's bound in paid employment he can't find?"

Roy smiled with sad eyes. "We're merely here for a cup of sugar."

"You want a bloody mug of it and the cake I've just baked," she seethed. "You lot and your bloody big society. Only thing that's big is the gap between me and you duck, just how you lot wanted it. Keep us at arm's length and under your bloody thumb with your tax, tax, tax. And now what is it you're bringing in just for us? Taxing our bloody bedrooms, that's what! You've even found a way to tax us whilst we sleep," and she grabbed hold of Kirty's hand, dragged her into the house, and shouted towards the small crowd at her front door. "It's my right to die in the house I was born in and I've two bedrooms in here, sir. Two!" - and she gave Roy and the TV cameras two fingers to prove her point then slammed the door.

"Bigot," sniffed Roy, as he made his way back to the car, unaware that the cameras were still rolling with beautiful PR.

Round 7

Joss Minton entered his local off-licence for a pint of milk. He wore his school uniform, his shirt un-tucked, the tie in his bag, the laces on his right shoe undone. It was not cool to wear a blazer and his jacket was a Nike cagoule, the zip long broken. There was only one other customer in the shop. That was Maggie Gifford. She was stood in front of the library of white wine in grey sweatpants considering her options: the 3-for-£10 offer on a vinegary Californian with a pretty label, or her usual box of Chardonnay reliable enough to numb her for a penny less.

What had happened earlier, Maggie couldn't quite remember. She recalled a small man, a large screwdriver, the Jobcentre staffroom with its fluorescent lights on full blast, and being offered a chair, a sweet cup of tea. *There you go. You sit yourself right there.* A copper who reeked of fags with a craggy worn face: he was going to come back and have a chat. Just got to go and do something first, call it seeing a man about a toolbox. No, no. You're safe. He's gone. Believe me duck, he won't be coming back. Not if I've got anything to do with it.

She'd been told to go home. Richard had made the call to the cab firm himself. Taken a tenner from his own wallet and said, "Go home Maggie. Come back Monday. We'll talk then about what to do." She hadn't been able to look Richard in the eye but had thought of him, naked in her bed, away with the fairies and out cold from the booze. She had grabbed his hand and pleaded, "Take me home, Richard. Please. I can't be on my own anymore." He had pushed the tenner into her hand and said *no. No. No.*

Maggie lifted her usual box of Chardonnay down from the shelf and hobbled over to the counter to pay for it. She had made her choice. She was given her change. She turned the penny over in her hand and then pretended it'd slipped through her fingers and dropped onto the floor without her noticing. She made to get on her way.

"Find a penny, pick it up, through the day you will get luck," Joss chanted, and bent down to retrieve the penny from the floor for her. "Give it to a friend and your luck will never end." He then handed it over.

"It's ok," said Maggie. "It's not mine."

Joss looked bemused. "Well, you know what they say," still holding the penny between his fingers. "Look after the pennies and the pounds will look after themselves."

"No they don't," she told him. "Pennies never do make pounds."

"Even so, it's still your money," and Joss was persistent.

"If it's bothering you that much son, you have it."

Joss watched her turn her back and make for the door. "Because I look like I need it?" and his tone could've chipped ice. "Because I look the type to be waiting for people like you to drop your fucking pennies on the floor?"

Maggie immediately thought she was being mugged. She looked back at the boy still holding her dropped penny then briefly at the guy behind the counter who was busy completing a stock report. The guy behind the counter chewed gum and seemed oblivious. She turned back to Joss and faced him.

"Do you know who I am?" she asked, throwing her shoulders back. "Have you any idea for who my son is?"

"That just assumes I give a fuck," Joss replied.

"I have no more money on me," she assured him, turning her jacket pockets inside out for him to see. "I came in with a tenner. I spent it. You have my change. And I'm too broke for credit cards. Look," she chucked her purse at him. "See? You and me aren't as different as you think."

Because always in arrears, always playing catch-up, the bailiff had come to explain to Maggie that she was so far in negative equity that even if she sold up right now, she wouldn't have enough to pay the bank back. She'd sunk into her sofa and asked, "What does that even mean?" and the bailiff had sat aside of her dunking Rich Tea she'd wished she'd not offered when even the plainest of biscuits were showing off riches she didn't have.

"It means you're worthless," he'd said. But he'd another idea, off the record and strictly between us. He had a friend called Malcolm Gandy with a big heart and a fat wallet who bought people's mortgages off them, furniture and fears included. "He'd buy your house then you rent it back off him. All contracted, all above board, lock stock, and no more money problems," and the bailiff had smiled flashing recent expensive dental work. "You think on," he'd said, and he'd reached for her hand: which she let him take and more because that's all she felt she was worth.

"You could put it in the charity pot if you're that bothered," Maggie told Joss, her head slightly cocked as she read the charity's name. "NSPCC," she said smiling. "How very apt," and she muttered a small "thank you" to no-one in particular and left the shop.

Joss looked down at the charity pot and found he was shaking. White scuffed plastic, string handle looking chewed, the green and white lettering of the charity's acronym on a peeling label; he wondered how many other people had dropped their pennies in the pot and how many pounds those pennies had made. He looked at the guy behind the counter engrossed in his stock take, chewing his gum. He edged towards the counter, reached out, swiped the pot, and legged it.

Round 8

Over in the playground facing the flats, just around the corner from the Jobcentre Plus, Jason Gifford threw a lit fag in the air to catch in his mouth. It didn't matter if it burnt his tongue. He'd been burnt before and that didn't hurt either. He was the only kid in the playground and he was sat on a swing rocking there and back, there and back, smoking his fag, gobbing on the asphalt, out early on good behaviour and enlisting in the playgrounds as if butter wouldn't melt.

He'd got nothing on him - he was a kid regularly pulled and searched – and he lit one fag from the other, flicked the dimp over the fence and headed over to the roundabout where he lay down, pulling his knees up towards his chest. As his teeth chatter in the late evening damp, a boy, no more than ten, approaches.

The boy wears a school uniform, the tie screwed up in his trouser pocket, and he's not been seen in school on a regular basis for three months. His shoelaces are undone and there are angry looking spots about his chin. Not because puberty beckons, but because he's had a two fingered Kit Kat for breakfast, a can of Coke, the rest of last night's chips. He chucks an envelope onto Jason's stomach. It feels too limp to be a full night's work.

Jason asks, "How much?"

The boy says, "Twenty."

Jason says, "Only twenty?"

The boy says, "I'm on a curfew and everyone's fucking skint."

Jason laughs.

The boy goes, "Don't fucking laugh at me, man."

But Jason does. He can't help it.

So the boy repeats himself. "I said, don't fucking laugh at me. You think I'm scared of you?"

"No."

"Then why are you fucking laughing?"

So Jason tells him. "Because you're still in fucking primary school and you think you're hard as fuck."

"I could rough you up no problem."

"And when you're fourteen you'll stab a mate with your Nan's bread knife and be far too high to know why." He chucks the envelope at the boy's feet. "Keep it," he says. "I'm sacking you off," and with another fag parked between his fingers, Jason throws his hood over his head and heads out of the playground, only pausing briefly to look down at a small man lying face down on the grassy knoll and sobbing.

Jason didn't ask if he was alright or for what he was doing down there, crying like a baby. He just thought pathetic, stepped over him, and made his way towards the park gates.

A police car drew up blocking his way, the driver's seat packed with a lumbering lump of uniform smoking a cigarette. PC Frank Blatch wound down the window. "When did you get out?"

"Nice to see you too, Frank."

Frank looks out of the windscreen. "You should go and see your mum," he says. "She's had a bit of upset at work today." Jason turns his back on the car and leans against it. "I mean it Jason. She's in a state."

No answer. Not a flinch. Frank gives him the sort of throaty chuckle that belongs to a man who makes dirty phone calls. "Such a big man aren't you?" he mutters. "And it takes a big man knock shit out of his mother."

"Your lungs are gonna need that sense of humour eventually," Jason replies, now leaning into Frank's window. "Give us a fag. Don't be tight."

Frank pulls out his Marlboro's and offers Jason the packet. He takes one and flicks open a Zippo.

"Nice lighter," Frank murmurs.

"Wallet was fucking priceless." Jason points down at a new pair of trainers.

Frank turns and squints in a spot of unannounced last sunshine. Then he points. "See that man over there on the grass crying his heart out?" Jason turns to look over at the man on the knoll. "He's been in a cell all his life. That what you really want?"

Jason pulls hard on the cigarette. He points up at the sky. "That's got a roof on it," he says. "Whole fucking world's one big cell," and he blows Frank a kiss and heads off in the wrong direction for home.

Frank looks over at Totty still curled up on the grass. He was surprised he was still there. He checks the time: almost seven. It was no wonder Constance had been calling him. "He's not come home Frank. It's been two bloody days." So Frank had done what he always did when Constance called. He'd turned left instead of right and had done so without so much as a thought for why. And as he'd continued going left, he'd put a call into his duty sergeant to say that he was stuck in traffic, possibly a pile-up, and he'd go and investigate. Except he'd got to Bennett Road quicker than he'd anticipated owing to every traffic light being on green and the roads being as quiet as the dead.

Constance had been in the kitchen flapping, washing the dishes, ordering Kirty to clean her teeth. Frank had kissed Kirty but not Constance and asked for where Joss was. "Gone to buy milk." Kirty was sent up to the bathroom to spit out her plaque. Constance had wiped her hands on her apron and told Frank, "I haven't seen him since Monday. Something's happened Frank. Something's not right."

Frank had sighed. Something had always happened. Something was always not right. He'd caught hold of Constance's arm and held it. "Connie," he'd begun.

She'd shrunk away from his grip and returned to the washing up.

"They just need a house Frank. And they'd only be borrowing it. Just until Totty gets things straight. You know these kiddies think the world of you." She'd turned and faced him, lowered her voice. "I haven't forgotten, you know. Your offer is always in the back of my mind."

Frank had moved closer towards her except Kirty was back now, bounding in pyjamas, brandishing sparkling teeth with one so wobbly the tooth fairy was on tenterhooks. She'd showed Frank with her tongue how her tooth hung "by a gum thread," and he'd scooped her up and told her that her tooth was worth its weight in gold. Then he'd nodded at Constance, said, "Ok, I'll go look for him," and slipped a two pound coin into her apron just in case that wobbling tooth disappeared in the night.

He'd hunted elsewhere before he'd returned to the park as a last shot. But now he was here and Totty was found, Frank couldn't actually be bothered to get out of the car.

"Always remember the dead stay dead." There it was again. Constance's voice, always, always in the back of his head, and then on that terrible day - 1st July 1978 - and after the police had finished with them all. "The mind plays such tricks when it's scared," Constance had explained to him, then a terrified thirteen year old who'd thought that they'd all just killed a boy. "It doesn't always remember what really happened so let me tell you for certain. Mally lost his footing and slipped into Jonty. You saw this and Totty saw it too." Constance had pulled them all together and rewritten what had happened. "You couldn't have done that and you didn't do that either, so don't ever say that you did Frank, because you didn't, do you understand?"

He had not understood but he'd said he did anyway. "I understand Connie." And from that day forth he'd made promises and pacts to always have Totty's back.

But for now, he put the car in reverse, left Totty where he was, still sobbing on their childhood knoll, and drove away.

Thursday 6th May

2010

Polling Day

Round 9

It's seven o'clock. Constance Minton comes down the stairs in her dressing gown to find her son catching flies in his armchair and reeking of cheap ale. She does not kick him awake as normal. Rather, she lets the storm brew up in the pot and even fries a few rashers of bacon with an egg. She pads towards the pantry, fetches out what's left of the loaf and adds a couple of slices to the pan. She cooks. She fries. She sighs. Her son doesn't even stir. She tips the whole lot on a plate and puts it down on the table. He can sort out his own condiments. Besides, she's out of ketchup, toothpaste and bleach for that matter. She pours herself a cup of tea – always in a cup and saucer for she was a potter through, through, and through – and sits down in the opposite armchair to study what she'd made.

She tells folk that he was born on 4th March 1966. That a few minutes after John Lennon told the world – "we're more popular than Jesus now" – God retaliated and gave us one Josiah John Edward Minton; a totty little blighter that was unlikely to make it through the night.

Constance was forty-five, torn and exhausted from over forty hours of labouring. Yet, she still managed to remove her son from his incubator with both hands. She clutched him between cold fingers that helped make her pastry so beautiful, and headed for a bed by the window where she lay and fed him constantly, whispering stories of what he'd come to be.

She told him that small boys grew into fine men, rich in friends with jobs for life. That she was a dipper and she'd married a placer. That her husband would bunch up her old stockings under his cap to form a pad so that he could carry the saggars into the oven upon his head. They'd bake. They'd go hard, just like his hands. He'd go back in; five overcoats and three jackets wrapped tight around his wrists. It was the only way, she told her son, for your father to lift those saggars down and bring them safely out into the world. Then he'd carry them away, like porcelain babes, and hand them over to the dippers who'd plunge them into love once more. "Josiah Spode was the only son of poor parents, but he still managed to perfect the art of fine bone china," as the first bars of the dawn chorus drifted into the hospital ward. And that's when Constance had begun to sob.

Because his feet would be ravaged by blisters, his left arm would become weaker than his right. His voice would chip rather than break and he'd stop growing at fourteen; hit his peak at 4ft 10 inches even when stood on tippy-toes. At fifteen he'd be dismissed from school as factory fodder. His teachers would use the word dim. He'd become a reliable lackey and sweeper of floors then play the troubled mistress to the teenage Lux Faithful, fall terminally in love with their kids. And though he'd never truly come to understand why turning the pages from left to right was wrong, that A was for apple and B was for ball, everyone needs a sweeper but not everyone can handle a broom, and though no-one is likely to lie on their death-bed wishing they'd swept more, without people like him the world would just get dirtier and the scum would start to breed.

Constance had stumbled to the payphone at the end of the hospital ward and fed it a few coins. It gave her enough time to tell Ned that she'd saved their son and to remember that size wasn't everything before the pips ran out. She'd mistaken Ned's silence for relief. But Ned, phone in hand and legs buckling, knew that he'd lost his wife to a totty little blighter that she'd go on saving until her own pips ran out and there was no more money for the slot.

*

Totty has begun to stir. "Where the bloody hell have you been?" Constance berates. "What in God's name have you been doing now?"

She sees that he's padded himself out in a couple of knitted jumpers, made several new bullet-holes in his father's work-belt to hold up a pair of old Sadlers' overalls that'd otherwise been trussed up with paperclips. He looks punched in the guts, as if he's been blinking away tears, and his left wrist is caked in his own blood.

"It's been two days, son," Constance raises her voice. "You promised me. You promised me no more."

Her eyes drift towards his feet, towards a blue metallic box that she's not seen before but that he's got chained to his left wrist where the metal loops have dug in and ripped through the skin. She taps at the box with a slippered foot. "What's that?"

Totty raises his better hand and runs it over his face like a cloth. He does not answer her.

She presses on. "What is it? A dog lead? Why? What's this all about?"

Totty waves her away and tells her not to start. Her response is to snatch down Ned's photograph and throw it onto his knees. "He went to war for you," she reminds Totty. "You're his son, his heir, his pride, so either you look him in the eye and tell him you've given up or you get back out there and you start to fight," and she pulls out of her pocket what was, to Totty, that piece of white paper that'd arrived for him a few days ago and which he'd opened and not read, but left stupidly on his bed for his mother to find. He didn't know all the words but he knew the logo and could read the signs. Lux was back.

"Social services," Constance waves the letter at him. "And you didn't think to tell me?"

Totty recalls taking a phone call. He pulls out his mobile from the top pocket of his overalls and squints at a cracked screen. Some bloke had called. Jack? Jock? Jake. Yes *Jake*. Lullaby voice. Half five if he remembers. He shrugs his shoulders at his mother and puts the phone back into his pocket. "Who cares?" he says. "I got custody."

"Grow up," Constance shouts. "And make sure you're here for those kids." She sits down at the table and pours more tea. She says, "It reeks of Malcolm, of course. He's no doubt paid Lux to do this because you won't accept any of his houses. Well, if it wasn't for me those kiddies would be in a home." To which Totty starts to groan.

Back in 1994, Constance can't remember the month exactly, Totty had brought home the girl who'd captured his heart and was still to give it back. She'd done tinned salmon sandwiches with salt and vinegar crisps and had to hold her tongue when Lux Faithful, with her salad cream hair and shortbread skin, hung onto Totty's arm with one hand, and held out the other to her as if she were royal. "It's Connie, isn't it? You like your boys to call you Connie, don't you?"

She was not yet seventeen but loomed over Totty, eleven years her senior, as if she'd seen and walked it all. What they had in common was nothing. Yet she was pregnant within the year.

She moved into Totty's back bedroom, painted the walls peach and fitted strips of mauve carpet with a staple gun. Then on a wintery Halloween's eve, they brought home their son called Josiah at Totty's insistence.

Lux said, "It's just a name."

Totty said, "It's not just a name. It's the name of my son."

By the time Joss turned three that's exactly who he was: he was Totty's son, for his mother was nowhere to be seen.

She came back four years later. Told Totty it'd all been their fault. They'd made her feel like she wasn't enough, that she wasn't doing it right. This parenting lark, she'd sobbed, it's so one-sided, so bloody crowded all the time. And then she cried some more and said no, she was wrong. She'd brought it all on herself. She deserved everything she'd got. She was pregnant again before Constance could get a word in edgeways. Totty picked mother and daughter up in a mini-cab that didn't quite make it to their front door. He'd only got a fiver in his back pocket.

"She's beautiful," the baby far too big for his hands. "She's just like her mother."

"No," said Lux. "She only looks like you."

Another four years passed. Lux went to the hairdressers to get her roots bleached but bottled it at the door. She never did come home after that.

"Can't you just love someone else?" Constance would ask, as she sliced up a freshly baked egg-custard, asked her son if he'd like it with cream.

"Nope," Totty would reply, and as was traditional, they'd leave it at that.

*

Constance hands Totty a mug of tea and alters her tone. "Whatever you're doing, son, it's not worth it. It won't make a blind bit of difference."

She breaks off. Not because she has run out of things to say but because it was a funny thing when it finally dawned on her that no mother truly knows what love is until she's had a son.

She moves closer, briefly touches his knee. It was practically a bear hug in their world.

"Did you see Frank?"

She's running water into a glass now, looking for aspirin in the cupboard drawer. "Did you ask him? What did he say?"

Totty adjusts himself in the chair. "He said no."

"Well, did you ask him properly? Did you tell him? Did you tell him what's going on?"

"He knows what's going on."

"And he said no?"

"Yes. He said no."

"You let him say no?"

"I am out there!" and Totty is exasperated. "I'm doing everything I can, everything I know to make them hear me. Believe me when I say it. I am out there!"

"And I won't be around forever," Constance replies. "I sometimes think you boys forget that," and she takes herself off into the front parlour where she thrusts open the curtains to let the morning light do its early alarm call, stopping only to rub at where she's just knocked up her shins on the corners of those ruddy camp beds.

Round 10

Rhonda is a cheaply-dressed fifty-something ex-social worker who's recently been redeployed by the council post its annual shuffle to cut costs. She now trains social workers to be, well, better at being social workers, and she's a conference regular, a textbook fanatic, and can fill a phone box with her chub and gristle and ginger ale skin. She is standing at the front of the room encased in flipcharts, a favourite visual aid of councils for this sort of training, and has set about creating a series of bullet points for discussion:

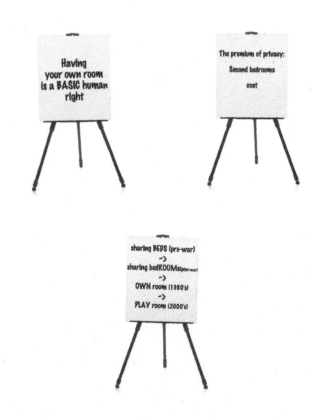

Rhonda believes it is vital for all children in social housing to have access to a bedroom where identity can be worked out and personalities forged. This doesn't necessarily mean a room of their own, but, at the very least, a definitive amount of space they can call their own and which is respected by others as their own. As Rhonda explains to anyone bothering to listen, the only reason kids hang out on street corners and join gangs is because they don't have an allocated private space at home where they can be themselves.

"And this is without us taking into account matters of gender and sexual orientation," with her arms flinging at her side. "Nine times out of ten the case is simply ashamed for how they live. And when they are, they exhibit one of three traits."

(She flips over the paper to a clean white sheet on the flipchart here, pulls off a pen lid with her teeth and starts to write)

1. Self-isolation, often seen in long-term delinquents where the body becomes the home.

2. Fantasy and make-believe - perceive themselves as someone else entirely who is much better off.

3. Worst case scenario: violent and aggressive behaviour brought on by envy and frustration for the lack of privacy they have in their lives.

"I see it a lot in teenage boys in particular," she adds, putting the lid back on the pen with her teeth.

To this, Jake groans. He is mildly hungover, has forgotten to clean his teeth, and is all the more tired and angry for the central heating being on. "It's that sort of middle-class guff along with the IKEA catalogue that makes people hound us for palatial property as a basic human right when there aren't enough houses to go round," drawing sniggers from those seated around him. "Magic the properties with a lick of paint on the walls, a radiator that works, no damp and everything *not* run on a meter and we might be getting somewhere where we need to be."

"And I remind you of the saying ...

...We've got to start listening to what these people really need."

"But you're not listening," Jake presses on. "This is about the council selling out to predatory landlords for a backhanding snip then having the nerve to send us lot in questioning when word gets leaked that they're living like dogs, packed in like sardines, poor as fucking crows. Have you any idea of what landlordism can do to a family who don't have the means to fight back?" And he's not to be interrupted now.

"Did you know that Malcolm Gandy owns over 60% of the social housing stock on our patch alone? That at least 80% of his rentals come from housing benefit and at least half of those are being trail-blazed by another one of his holding companies for what he's calling rent on headcount and the under-occupation of the elderly. That, to my mind, is a lot of state money lining his pockets. Yet, I don't see no scaffolding replacing the   roof tiles on

Trent Street, or new central heating systems in the flats up The Towers. And as for the installation of water meters and how he fixes them to cost more than the average utility bill, well." He exhales loudly. "He should be as clean as a pin."

"That's because he bathes every night in a sweet smelling soap he's got shares in," says Ursula, slow-clapping his speech from the back of the room. "But bravo Povey, my brave little soldier, bravo."

"Don't mock me," Jake snaps. "Half those kids on Trent Street can't even sleep in their bedrooms for the damp and you're making me sit here and listen to this guff?"

"And you can huff and puff all you like, but you won't blow his houses down now," and Ursula sniggers. "We'll have a new government by morning Povey and mark my words, since they'll be very anti-social and very pro the landlord what exactly do you propose we do when the Tories start to drain the public sector pot dry?"

"Help," Jake says. "Fight on. Build the houses ourselves!"

Ursula smiles. "Povey, Povey, Povey," getting up from her chair to leave. "If only we all gave as much of a shit as you did about picking up the rubbish around here. What a wonderful world it would be." And though she had left the door open for Jake to follow her dissent, he decided that, for now, he'd remain in the room with his fellow mug and suffer a little more.

Round 11

Pete's badge says he's "happy to help". He thrusts his arm out and nods that-away, "Eight aisles down on the right, that's where all your paint is lad," and his eyes lock onto what looks like a toilet-chain that's strapped around Totty's left wrist. He follows it all the way down to the toolbox that hangs about his ankles like a knackered up mutt.

Totty hands Pete the colour chart and points. "Do you have this colour?"

Pete reads the label and tells him, "Probably."

"Could you show me?"

Pete isn't best pleased. He'd spent thirty-three years behind a thick glass pane in Barclays bank; a junior clerk who made it to senior cashier and who was happy as Larry until redundancy took him by the short and curlies and forced him to downsize to a bungalow before downsizing became fashionable. Now, he's bitter and he is sore and he knows nothing about DIY. At fifty-eight, he'd rather be retired with his feet up, slippers on, Racing Post, but neither his pension nor wife will allow it.

He nods at Totty and sets off with the most spirited of strides, forcing Totty to take up some sort of jog-trot behind him. He walks straight up to the paint Totty wants and, noting this customer's shortcomings, takes the tin down from the shelf.

"This is the colour?"

Pete, his eyebrows creasing, nods.

"You're sure it's the right pigment? I'm not going to get back home and find it's the wrong one?"

Pete hands the colour chart back to Totty and assures him that this is the colour.

"Could you open it?" Totty asks. "Let me check inside, see the colour for myself?"

Pete frowns. "Afraid not," he says, "company policy," and, with an apologetic tilt of the head, he starts to walk away.

Totty calls after him. "Mate, don't walk away. Do us a favour and just lift the lid for a second, let me check the colour."

Pete stops and turns. "You'll have to go and pay for it first."

Totty sighs and runs a hand through his hair. "I'm not shelling out for a tin of paint before I know it's the right colour," he says. "Just open the tin for me. No-one's looking. I don't see what the fucking problem is."

"There is no problem," and Pete clears his throat. "I've just told you it's company policy."

"That's just middle-class code for having to be a twat," Totty sniffs. "And yet you're the one wearing the fucking apron."

Pete, a reserved and docile man who hated confrontation of any kind, is both startled and annoyed. He holds onto a bantering tone. "Civility will cost you nothing and I'd prefer it if you'd mind your language. There might be women and children shopping in the next aisle."

Totty looks about him. "Civility," he echoes accusingly. "You're talking to me about civility? Are you kidding me?"

Pete keeps his eyes locked on Totty. "Look," he begins. "I don't quite know what it is you're trying to start here."

"Do you even know what the fucking word means?"

"Again," and Pete tilts his head as if he's straining to hear, "the swearing, sir, is really not necessary."

"But you want me to be civil to you, right? Man to man, here on the shop floor?"

Pete opens his mouth but no words form.

"Because this is a civil society, right? All of us living shoulder to shoulder under one roof? So why are you slumming it and wearing my apron?"

"Pardon me?" and Pete even looks down at the branded black and orange apron he is wearing.

"You're wearing my apron, *sir*. And you're wearing it because you trusted the banker. You thought he'd make you money. You thought you could be one of them. You thought you deserved to be one of them. I want holidays and cars and houses just like them. Well, that's where your middle-class civil society has got you, sir. You might've worked your arse off for forty odd years and saved like a trooper, but you're no further up the food chain than lifting a tin of paint off the top fucking shelf in B&Q for an illiterate short-arse who can't reach his dreams," and Totty pulls out his claw hammer from his back pocket. "I know who *I* am, but do you?"

Pete steps back. Pete even points his finger. "That mate, is threatening me. That's harassment," and he begins to slowly back away down the aisle.

Totty looks confused. "What are you talking about?" twirling the hammer in his hand so that the rubber-grip end is being handed to Pete. "I just want you to open that tin of paint, though you'd love to have a go, wouldn't you? I can see it in your eyes," and he taps the side of his left temple with the hammer-head. "I'm game," he taunts. "But you swing first big man. You can even wipe your hands on my apron when you're done."

But Pete has begun to run; security will be called, and the next thing Totty will know is that he will be hauled into a barely furnished whitewashed room, his hammer classed as an offensive weapon threatening a member of staff.

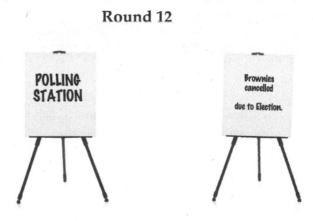

The Community Centre local to Bennett Road was not enjoying a good turnout of voters despite their offer of tea and cake while-u-wait. Constance was, in fact, the only person in there other than Mavis Browning and her daughter Bryony who were sat behind a table covered with a red paper cloth - *no bias, Connie, not at all* - and one large ballot box that Mavis cradled like a child. It was also chained to the table leg. Votes could get robbed, Mavis explained to Constance, handing her a voting slip and then a pencil which she'd got Bryony to sharpen. "And you look a bit peaky, Connie. You suffering a bit?"

"Mind you own business," Constance sniffed, as she took the paper and pencil and made her way into one of the booths at the back of the hall, where she slumped against the ledge and closed her eyes. Goodness that jabbing pain in her chest was sharp! It must've been something she'd eaten. And what, with getting all wound up with Totty this morning and that social worker due: it was no wonder she frazzled her nerves.

She looked down at the slip of paper to distract her from the second jolt of pain that socked her in the breast, and for the first time in a long time she wondered which box to tick.

"Vote with your heart, Connie," a voice whispered, and she turned around, covering the paper with her hand as if sitting an exam.

"Frank. You frightened the life out of me!" She placed a hand on her breast and held it there for awhile, if nothing more than to dispel the pain that was cutting into her.

"Sorry." He smiled, putting his hand on her shoulder for as long as he dared. "You ok?"

"For goodness sake, what is it with you all today?" She pushed away his hand and turned her back on him to tick the one box she always ticked. Then she turned to look at Frank.   "Will you let me out?"

He moved in closer. "Connie," he began.

"There's nothing wrong Frank. I'm old, that's all. And old is not easy. You'll find out soon enough." She held up her hands as if defending herself.

"You're not old Connie."

"I am Frank. *Too* old."

"Not for me."

She screwed up the voting slip in her hand absent-mindedly. "Frank."

"I don't mean it like *that*," he was saying to her. "It's not like *that*. You know that. I just, well. You know." He stopped to look down at his shoes. She followed his gaze and saw how dirty his boots were. A man without pride left the house in shoes like that. A man without care and a wife.

"You're a good boy Frank," she told his shoes.

"I'm forty-six years old Connie. We all grew up long ago."

"Did you?" and she looked him straight in the eye. "Sometimes I think none of you did. You're all making a bloody mess of it."

This made him take her hand. "But I have money Connie and you still keep saying no."

"And it's still no."

He backed out of the booth a little and shook his head. "You're just scared," he said. "But I'd stop all that. You, me, the kids. Think of *them*. Isn't that what you keep telling me?"

She shook her head and tried to smile. "There *is* someone else out there for you Frank."

"It's not like *that* Connie. I just want... I wish I could explain... you... *you* did this. You made me need only you."

Constance looked down at the screwed up voting slip in her hand. She tried to smooth out its creases, smiling up at Frank now and then, and telling him that he was home, Totty. He'd come home but was in no great shape, and that she worries, naturally; it's her job to do so, you understand Frank. You know how it is. And then she said, "Oh!" and "Oh no!" and she pushed Frank aside and headed back to Mavis and Bryony. "I need another slip," she said. "I've made a mistake on this."

Mavis shook her head. "I'm sorry Connie. But that's your vote."

"Don't be ridiculous. Give me another one."

"No can do Connie. You've had your chance."

"But look!" said Constance, showing Mavis her voting slip. "I've voted for Roy bloody Dingwall. I don't want to vote for Roy Dingwall. I've made a big mistake."

Mavis looked horrified. She clamped her hand dramatically over her eyes and instructed Bryony to do the same. "Don't show us how you've voted," she snapped. "You're not supposed to tell. It's against the law and we're impartial."

"But it's the wrong box! Come on Mavis. Bryony. Give me another slip. What's wrong with you both?"

"It's not the rules, Connie. The rules say one vote per person."

"And I haven't voted yet, have I? Frank!" she called him back. "Tell them. You're a police officer. Tell them that I'm not breaking any law in asking for another slip."

Frank wandered over with his hands in his pockets. "Look," she showed Frank. "I've ticked Roy Dingwall and he's not Labour anymore, is he? Now these pair won't let me have a new slip. Tell them. Tell them it's not against the rules when you've made a mistake. Sort it will you, Frank? Please?"

Frank looked down at Constance and for a long time said nothing. He could sort this out. He would sort this out. He sorted out a lot and always for them. Because *you did this. You made me need only you.* He had said it, hadn't he? And she had heard him but said nothing. Not no. Not yes. And here she was, sniggering, nervously, as if he were a figure of fun to her to poke and prod. "Don't be too prosperous now, Frank," she used to warn. "You'll attract the wrong sort of woman." He thought of all the passed-up carrots dangled because of her: promotion, management, a few more hundred in his pocket, make it a couple of thousand. *Come on Frank. This job's got your name written all over it!* "No, you're alright," he'd say. He did not ever want her to hate him, to balk at his success.

She was prompting him again. "Frank. Tell them please. Tell them how I've just made a mistake!"

But it was he who had made the mistake.

He looked down at his shoes. "I'm sorry Connie. For everything I've just said and for everything you think I might not have done for you." He took a few steps away from her then turned and ran.

Constance screwed up her face and called after him. "Frank! What on earth... Oh, here... just give me a minute...." and she gave the slip of paper to Mavis and hurried after Frank. "Frank. Wait! Frank!" And Mavis looked at Bryony and Bryony looked at Mavis and eventually Mavis, being the braver of the two, popped Constance's voting slip into the ballot box.

"Who'd have thought it, eh?" Mavis giggled. "Constance Minton voting blue."

Round 13

Jake had heard a lot about this road, the family that lived at its fag-end. It was hard not to. The consultation process had been front page news for the bulk of last year: the story no longer just a story but a city saga owing to the various public floggings of Town Hall reputations over the sale of Bennett Road. Town planners had vehemently denied that it was anything but government driven – "policy for social housing. Council is a derogatory term" - whilst local councillors, in tweed slacks and loosened ties, professed over double brandies that it was proxy of a land sale to the not-for-profit Gandy & Gandy Associates UK who had agreed, in a 400 page legal document (available online), to regenerate this last batch of council houses, subject to planning permission, under Malcolm Gandy's usual wheeze of localism, localism, localism.

However, just before Christmas, Bennett Road was reported to have been sold not to Gandy & Gandy Associates UK, but to MG Homes Plc. This had meant two things.

1. 90% of Bennett Road had accepted handsome part-exchanges in return for flitting within 30 days, rendering this blunt stretch of road (almost) empty and (nearly) ready to be turned into a signature Gandy galley of bed-sits, upstairs and down.

2. A 40% stake of MG Homes Plc sat with shareholders, many of whom sat on council benches looking to bolster their pension pots since the expenses scandal had left a shortfall in their incomes. Not only did this beg the question - just how much money was really spent on these old bricks - but called for the nuts of the vendor who'd authorised such a backdoor gazumping.

Whilst all this was going on "up town," the Mintons had taken root and an awful lot of umbrage against the man who'd long referred to their house as "my true home." Malcolm Gandy had not only grown up as part of their furniture, but made a slew of pacts with the family along the way. His insistence for them to move out and be treated like everyman else had not only hit Totty sideways, but hurt Constance's feelings to the point that she was within snivelling distance of producing an actual tear.

She had even appealed for help during the Lost and Found feature on local radio and was visited the next day by an employee of the Citizen's Advice Bureau with a sludge of inky black hair, a big old file, and a slight limp. He had explained to Constance that if the general community agreed that Gandy's redevelopment plans drastically improved what already stood, then so be the regeneration, but only on the understanding that the council evicted their own tenants on the grounds of unsuitability. "They must also offer a proper notice period and an alternative property that comes up to the legal standards they say Bennett Road no longer complies to," he'd said.

"But it's my home," Constance had said in reply, and she'd asked the man to come to the window. "Look," she'd instructed, lifting the net. "Do you see them? Cups and saucers, teapots and plates, everything the world needed and somewhere the world came to when they needed them. This is where the people lived who made them. And if they didn't like making them at one factory, they walked across the road to another, started that afternoon and made some more. Do you see?"

"What I see," the young man had said between slurps of milky tea. "Is mass redundancy Mrs Minton, and enough loopholes for any new company not to honour the original terms of the contract." He'd straightened the net at the window on Constance's behalf. "It's not entirely illegal but it is unjust." And he'd advised Constance to assume squatter's rights.

"I can do more than that," she'd replied, because as luck would have it, they'd also got a little bit of history on their side.

"Malcolm Gandy killed a boy, you know," Constance would tell any unassuming passer-by, "and only got away with it because of us."

But every catastrophe has its lifespan and, five months on, no-one was at all interested in what Constance Minton still had to say about the man who'd invested hard and vast in an otherwise rotten area in the name of home improvement.

In fact, *whatever*, some said, when she dragged up the Minton - Gandy history. Little boys drown all the time, and besides, with a lick of Gandy's paint, that end of terrace of theirs won't half look plush.

As for Jake, his first impressions of 13 Bennett Road was that if security and stability were fundamental, then however did people find it in shitholes like that?

Round 14

Joss and Kirty Minton were sat at the kitchen table waiting for their new social worker to arrive. Joss poked his tongue out at his sister. She poked out hers in reply.

"Round nose," he goes.

"Big chin," she went.

"We don't have to go anywhere we don't want to," he said. "Mum can't make us and neither can they."

"I know what I have to say," Kirty assured her brother, frightened of nothing and no-one. "I can look after myself."

"But that's my job," Joss told her. "You know that's what I do," and she nodded because she did.

"It's all about us," she said.

"Yes," said Joss. "It's only ever about us," and he leant across the table and nipped at her funny bone to make her giggle.

Josiah Edward Fenton Minton was beginning to grow into his adult skin. Already nudging six foot with size 13 feet, he had the sort of corn-yellow hair girls went to salons for with skin as smooth as dinner-plates. Constance feared he was too handsome and did all she could to keep him fifteen. Constance liked children to be children, and for a long time after too. But Totty disagreed. Joss was outgrowing them and clever kids were better off being clever elsewhere. No-one liked a clever-dick round here. "I was held back by the pack," Totty always insisted, handing his mother his dirty washing. "Until the pack gave up on the runt to survive."

Kirty Lux Lavender Minton had not long turned seven. It hadn't been her intended name. Rather, the woman up the Town Hall who'd registered her birth had had her mind on other things, and because

73

Totty had been unable to read her mistake on the birth certificate, the name had stuck out of respect. It didn't matter. She was always someone else anyway.

She was now at the kitchen sink playing shipwrecks. All the cutlery were swimming for their lives. "Save yourselves," she shouted at the knives and forks. "This is your Captain speaking. Swim for your life and hold on." Playing natural disasters was her favourite thing to do before social workers knocked at the door.

Kirty dried her hands on a tea-towel then pulled out her magnifying glass from her trouser pocket. She looked over at her brother with one elongated pupil. "It's a fishy business," she said. "I can say with some completion that we're all going to hell."

"Then I think you should take that wig off before we get there," referring to the bob-length tinsel wig she'd worn home from school having found it in the dressing up box in another classroom.

"But I'm in disguise," she replied. "I didn't want Mum to see me."

"Was she there?"

"She's always there."

"You never said. Where was she?"

"You didn't ask."

"Well, I'm asking now. Was she there?"

"Nope."

Joss scowled and made to grab the wig. Kirty squealed. "No! It'll make it look like I'm having fun."

"You *are* having fun."

"Not all the time. Sometimes, you make me think about serious things."

"But only for five minutes. Then you can have fun again," and because she'd made no attempt to remove the wig, Joss leant across the table and pulled it away from her head.

"Give it back!"

"No. And don't play up when he gets here either. Be *you*."

"I am me."

"I mean it Kirty."

She still wailed her indignation. She did not like to be told. "Can I cartwheel?" she asked.

"No."

"Not even one?"

"No."

"But I can cartwheel better than anybody."

"That's not why he's coming Kirt."

"Because we sleep sick, right?"

"We don't sleep sick. And don't ever say that in front of Nan. She'll wash your mouth out with soap and water."

"Brilliant! I can blow bubbles at him!"

"Kirty. I mean it!"

"Don't tell Nan *what*?" Constance hurried into the kitchen and glared up at the clock. Joss followed her gaze, shook his head, then looked back at the table.

Kirty managed to squeeze in, "Joss says we sleep sick," but her brother spoke over her too loudly for Constance to really hear.

"He was never going to be here," he said, shaking out the tangles in the tinsel wig. "You put too much hope in him and that's why he lets you down."

"It's nothing to do with it," and Constance, back from the

community hall, looked both hassled and subdued. "Your mother is a very vindictive woman and Malcolm Gandy wants to remember who we are." She removed her headscarf. "If his father was still alive to see what kind of man he'd become..."

"Does he sleep sick too?" Kirty butted in. Constance glared at Joss.

"What have you been saying now?"

"Nothing," with his head in his hands. "She's just being Kirty." He paused. Constance still wore *the look*. "What do you want me to say? Mum's this, mum's that. She's here. Then she's not. God, all I remember is looking at her back."

Tugging at her tights as she washed the dishes and argued with his daddy about going out; tapping at her ankles with a wooden spoon whilst she looked out of the bedroom window crying at the clouds; Lux stood at the hallway mirror, putting on her face, doing her hair, "Aren't I the prettiest mummy Jossy? Don't I look pretty for you?" Telling her calves he'd like a biscuit, "I'm hungry mummy." "Well, I'm not and your tummy's smaller than mine and you don't want a big belly do you?" And she'd carry on chatting on the phone, smoking her cigarettes, gassing with friends; "Get off me Jossy, I'm working. Go and play."

Then she was gone.

Then she was back.

Then she was gone again.

She came back for a longer time and had a baby with her who took up all her time.

He asked her back, "Don't you like me anymore?"

She said, "Shhh. The baby's sleeping," and spooned the baby with her back to him like he never remembered her spooning him.

He was twelve when she left them for good. Twelve years, five months and sixteen days.

He got angry at first. Was punished with a lot of detentions and a couple of suspensions and got allocated a social worker who made him chuck all his anger in a big metal bin that he could, when the time came, set fire to.

He did. Just outside of the art cabin. A gust of wind did its worst. All those unfinished works of art. He got expelled.

He went to Blurton High and moved onto envy. Everyone had something he wanted. Gadgets, gizmos, girls, guts. He found things in his school-bag and didn't know why they were there.

Then came a year of apathy. He wagged. He bunked. He skipped half the year until an education welfare officer cut him a deal. Pull your finger out clever-dick or we'll place you out of borough into care. So he did. He flew through the next year courting A's and Libby Lymer until her mum found them half-dressed and called the police. Virginity lost (sort of, as much as these things can be), he knuckled down and bare-knuckle fought anyone who dared call him a swot.

He had twelve GCSE-s to sit and heart-throb status as the pin-up for the sink. Yet Joss Minton couldn't put his finger on why he'd swiped that charity pot from the off-licence counter. It was a low act, the lowest of the low, and yet he felt so empty about doing it.

He hoped that the pot would just disappear. Disintegrate. Then he could forget it was ever there. He thought about where to leave it, stash it, hide it. So he wouldn't have to live with it. But it still remained at the bottom of his school rucksack. Unopened plastic. NSPCC. Same as it was when he'd swiped it.

He slapped at his cheeks. Pulled on his ears. Pinched at his skin. Ragged his own hair. But nothing. He still felt nothing. He reached for a fork on the kitchen table and without thinking for his sister sat upon her grandmother's knee, he stabbed at his right arm. No blood. No pain. He felt numb. A boy who robs a charity pot was already dead inside.

"What the hell are you doing?" Constance snatched the fork from his hand.

"It's just a house," he shouted. "We don't become someone else just because we have to live somewhere else. We're still the same people. I mean, why don't we just go? It's a bigger house. We all get rooms. What's the big deal?"

Constance's eyes narrowed. "What *bigger* house?"

"This house that Gandy's offered Dad," he began without thinking. "We only have to live there on paper and then maybe, just maybe, everyone will leave us alone."

"But a house not too big," Kirty interjected, leaving her grandmother's knee with one unfinished plait. "I might get lost in a big house. I might not know where everyone is," and she picked up the remote control, pointed it at the small portable telly that sat atop of the fridge and said to Joss, "Deal or no deal big chin?"

And he said, "No deal, round nose, but thanks for the offer," and she jumped onto his knee to settle in just in time for the opening credits.

Round 15

Jake Povey sat at Constance's kitchen table and wouldn't take a cup of tea. A cup of tea might tell a thousand stories but it could also pass on a million bugs. He'd even sneered at Constance's offer of a mug of Mellow Bird's. Constance thought this slovenly and perhaps even a little rude. Eventually, she persuaded him to accept a thin slither of her Victoria Sponge and a glass of water to wash it down; Constance letting the tap run for awhile not wishing a tepid glass to cloud his judgement on how she kept house.

Whilst she did, Kirty informed Jake that they were having boiled eggs for dinner with soldiers that marched head first into yolk. That they'd had pork chops for tea last night, there were yoghurts in the fridge, and if he looked inside the teapot he'd see the tealeaf thief clinging onto the teabags like a raft. "But don't worry," she assured Jake. "He'll survive. He always does."

She introduced him to her big brother Joss then, saying, "He'll happily peel the skin off a slug, you know," and Jake raised his eyebrows and said, "Really? How cruel," then he checked his watch and asked Constance if he might take a look upstairs.

"Why on earth do you need to see up there, Mr Povey?"

"I'll make it as quick as I can," was how he eventually decided to answer her question.

"You know, in my day," Constance began, as she led Jake down the hall (deep burgundy wallpaper, velour to the touch) towards the stairs, "most people in this road didn't have a penny to rub against a wart." She stopped at the bottom step and gave him a nasty look. "Then some sons were no good, some daughters were up to no good, most husbands drank their pay packets and most wives could slug it out better than any man when they needed a loaf, but the state never came round to tell us lot how to live."

Jake cleared his throat. "It's a world of ideals now Mrs Minton," he said. "We're all looking for some sort of ideal and to know that the kids are alright."

Constance dismissed this as flannel. Her kids were fine – that's right, *fine.*

"But they're not your kids are they Mrs Minton?"

Constance pursed her lips. "I've mothered all my life, Mr Povey. It's all the same where I've come from," and she eyed him suspiciously.

He was broodingly blue-eyed and awkwardly postured, over six foot yet dramatically underweight. There was a gentleness to him that suggested understanding, generosity, perhaps even touching on shame. Or he was just slack - Constance really couldn't be sure – and she placed him as late thirties almost forty (flecks of grey hair), probably single (his shirt wasn't ironed), and as disillusioned with the state (no tie or suit jacket) as he was at loggerheads with the system he represented (scuffed shoes, no briefcase, stubble). He was, she decided, simply lost.

She took him upstairs as slowly as she could, ensuring that he had the time to admire the gallery of family photographs along the way. She told him that some were still living but most long dead, and she hoped that he'd ask her some questions, give her a little time to catch her breath and jiggle about her ankles to get the blood flowing again. The pain was particularly antagonising today. She'd been sick in her handkerchief three times. That was twice more than yesterday. And the colour had been alarming.

Constance paused at the top of her stairs. A two-up, two-down terrace with an upstairs bathroom was, back in the day, very la-di-da, and Constance was terribly proud that she went *up* to the loo as she still went *up* to bed. She pushed open the bathroom door and stood aside allowing Jake to take a look. A frosted glass window, clean towels on a rail, a bolt on the door, four toothbrushes in a pot, and plenty of toilet-roll stashed to the side of the bath. He could smell bleach, lots of it, and Pears soap.

"You know, these bedrooms aren't really any of your business Mr Povey," and Jake caught sight of a slight pinking in both her cheeks. "You do realise that if I open these doors to you, you will take the last scrap of privacy I have left?"

Jake wished he'd something else in his hand other than his notepad. "I know how you must feel Mrs Minton..."

"No you don't Mr Povey. You're putting the size of a house before the welfare of the family inside it."

Jake looked at the two shut bedroom doors. "Mrs Minton. I am trying to make this as inoffensive as I can."

"Then go back down the stairs," she told him. "The children are not up here."

"But the more you refuse to let me in, the more I'll become suspicious of their contents." He looked at Constance standing protectively in front of her bedroom door. "You've allowed me this far," he reminded her.

"What is it that you think you're going to see in an old woman's bedroom?" And she held his gaze for as long as she could stand. "No man has been in this room since my husband died. Not even my son goes in there."

"I still need to look."

"Then you people really have taken everything from me," and she moved aside and sat at the top of the stairs.

13 Bennett Road was a house truly full of Constance Minton. She cluttered up every room. She hung at every window. Flick a switch and she was stood there looking for dust. Except for her son's room that is, and Jake couldn't put his finger on why he felt so uneasy about being in there. It was, after all, what he'd come to see, and it reeked of a lodger who didn't pay his way. Other than the single bed, there was a small black cabinet where two washed out photographs of two babies had been taped together in a single frame, a mug of tea stood

aside of it, stone cold. He was a man with nothing and nothing more than this. Perhaps all this nothing was all that he needed. Perhaps he kept nothing in order to slip away. A man with this sort of nothing barely existed, and Jake felt so very sorry for being in there at all.

"We've never missed a rent payment, you know," said Constance, interrupting Jake's thoughts. "Not since the day we were handed the keys in 1937. We should own it outright by rights, must've paid for it twice over, and yet we tell ourselves that we don't have that sort of money. That owning was what ruined the likes of us. And it did divide us, Mr Povey, made some of us think that we were better than the rest. But I couldn't own, and certainly not without Ned," and she offered up a small smile. "Malcolm Gandy will sub-let this house you know," she told him. "Upstairs to one family, downstairs to another, and yet here you are quibbling about the indecency of camp-beds," and she thumped a bony little fist on the bedroom door. "But then he has money Mr Povey. He can do what he likes."

Jake stepped out of Totty's room and pulled the door behind him. "Where is Mr Minton right now?" he enquired.

"He couldn't get off work early," Constance told him quickly. "He tried, but he couldn't, though I will, of course, tell him that you're rooting for him. He'll be so relieved to know that you're on his side," and she made her way down the stairs, a lot more flustered than she would've cared to have shown.

Jake followed gingerly, utterly astonished that everything in the old woman's bedroom had been pink.

Round 16

Malcolm Gandy had always kept a keen eye on this particular batch of 1960-s three-bed semi's just shy of the Leek Road. Maggie Gifford's had oblong windows that took a gull's fancy, utility, Venetian blinds, and she'd come here as a newly-wed back when newly-weds and new houses began to call themselves middle-class. But now, after her husband's on-the-sly re-mortgage that had left her unable to meet the monthly repayments, the bank had lost its rag and Maggie needed a cash sale rush-job with few questions asked.

Gandy reckoned he could get his hands on the place for at least £20,000 less than it was worth on account of wood rot and sheer desperation. He patted his paunch and entered smiling knowing that he'd get this little goldmine on the market within six weeks, perhaps make his money back twice over by Christmas. Then he saw the state of her kitchen and his heart burst apart.

A door-less oven and grease-spattered walls, every inch of her kitchen worktops were covered with something sticky, something nibbled, whilst stacks of crockery, still making their way to the sink, were encrusted with baked beans and three-day-old-oats. He smelt cat litter and disinfectant - one sprayed to disguise the other - the whiff from three large pizza boxes left atop of the pedal bin since Sunday snatching at his breath. It was a hovel. It was beyond belief, and in all the years he'd been eyeing up houses, Malcolm Gandy had never witnessed one so in need of a man's touch.

Out of the corner of his eye, he could see that Maggie was shaking as she tried to make tea and fumbled about for clean mugs. She looked heavily mortgaged about the eyes, as if her trouser suit had been bought with spare change, and she was wearing these silly red-heeled boots, her flesh bunched where the zips wouldn't fasten like they should.

"Or there's wine," Maggie told Gandy as she opened the fridge, and he watched her remove a box of Stowell's Chardonnay then hunt out glasses from a dishwasher. She handed him a thumb-smudged glass of corky white and tipped her own glass in his direction. Gandy's lips grazed the rim; the smell telling him not to drink.

"I know what you're thinking," she said. "But I warned him when his Dad left. I said 'there's no law against me not lifting a finger either, so it's your choice Jason. We both play mother or we don't'," and she smiled, tipped more wine inside her and headed back to the box for a top-up.

The living area was no better and there was no separate dining room either. Just one room knocked through to the other creating a living space too big to be homely, too stark to look properly used. They'd not been a family to congregate around a table. "Have you ever tried to get two men to sit down at a table with you, appreciate what you've taken the time to cook and *talk*?"

But Gandy didn't do personal questions. Houses were his family. Bricks one big adventure. And he busied himself with a tape measure, striding across the long room measuring its length, width and depth. He pointed at the woodchip on the walls.

"I know," and Maggie shook her head. "Another thing we never got round to doing."

"Just that you'll be paying for it now," Gandy told her.

"I don't ever expect anything today not to hit my pocket," washing her opinion down with more wine.

"So we *are* moving then?" and Maggie swung round to find Jason had put in an unexpected appearance, his voice at a level that suggested there was a pecking order he was keen for Gandy to acknowledge.

"It's just a valuation," and Maggie glowered at her son. His unbelted jeans were his style statement, his straggling hems covered in muck. He held a half-smoked joint between his fingers, had a lighter parked up behind his ear. He was sweating. He smelt stagnant. He looked as if he wanted to punch her lights out, perhaps even finish her off. The hatred, thought Gandy, was a feeling he knew only too well.

"Sounds like you're fucking giving us away," Jason replied. "Or maybe it's just how much you value yourself."

Gandy took out his own cigarettes and tapped one against the box. "You want to engage your brain sunshine before you let that sort of talk devalue a house," he warned. "Talk like you're from a shithole and I'll give you a shithole's price." He held the cigarette towards Jason, gesturing for a light. Jason took the cigarette, pulled his lighter out from behind his ear, and lit it for himself. He inhaled rough and deep.

"She'll try and fuck you, you know," he smirked grubbily. "It's how she pays for everything round here."

"Haven't you got homework or something?" and Maggie's voice was so very little. Gandy sniffed around the boy's jacket.

"Got a problem mate?" Jason asked.

"Maggots," Gandy said eventually. "You're quite the piece of shit aren't you?" and then he turned to Maggie and asked if he might view her upstairs.

Maggie rattled away at Gandy as if her son was just another utility bill that came with the house. "Years ago a factory would've had him. Someone would've made him their apprentice. Found room for him in their van." She seemed to find this funny. "He's not the only one though. I work at the Jobcentre. I see them every day. All jittery eyes and beaten-up looks, and I can't magic the jobs for them. They think I can. They think I should. Then they're that pissed off that I can't they even threaten me with a hammer. They never stop to think that I don't have it so good either, and there's nothing worse than being made to feel guilty for working, Mr Gandy. Though I'm sure you don't."

Gandy turned away from her and tried a door behind him. It was locked.

No. That room was private. It was Jason's room and she didn't have a key.

"There's nothing in there," she said. "I made sure of that."

And there wasn't. Maggie had long thrown out all of Jason's possessions when he was inside; four months in a juvenile detention centre somewhere in the North West and near the coast. Smashing views, turrets covered in ivy; she'd been driven there by a gruff-dressed social worker called Jake Povey with a lullaby voice in an old battered Fiat with only one working windscreen wiper. They'd arrived after a ghastly four-hour journey and she'd not been able to go in. It was her fault he was in there – she'd shopped him, had him taken down – and she'd spent the allocated three visiting hours sat in the car chain-smoking and swigging from a hipflask of gin.

Jake had returned to her an hour later and said he thought it was doing him good. "He'll come back to you a changed man," he assured.

But Jason had returned home and looked at his mother as if she was a highly contagious disease.

"I had no choice," Maggie had told him, as he'd kicked off his trainers – another new pair of trainers - and rooted in her handbag for her fags. "Put yourself in my position Jason. You might even do the same thing yourself one day. I had no choice."

"Oh you had a choice," he'd sneered, removing his socks. "You just chose fucking badly. Again." And then he'd gone upstairs to his room, come back down and kicked off. "Where's all my stuff? What the fuck have you done with all my stuff?"

"I wanted you to come home and start anew," Maggie had cried from behind her hands. "I want nothing of the old Jason in my house."

But the old Jason had never gone away and that's why he knocked her to kingdom come wearing his new trainers as boxing gloves.

Maggie took Gandy into her bedroom then, stood behind him as he measured up and checked the view from the window. The type of people he wanted to rent this place didn't like to be overlooked, didn't want to neighbour just *anyone*, and didn't like fitted wardrobes that made bedrooms look like caravans either. He turned round to ask Maggie if the mirrored wardrobes could be unscrewed from the wall and saw that she'd wasted no time; had unbuttoned her blouse and was unclipping her bra. Her breasts, when unleashed, were two mighty things, and although Gandy wasn't entirely adverse to them, he preferred a less vacuum-packed set of tits.

"What are you doing?"

He looked for something to cover her up, eventually settling upon a damp bath-towel he'd found slung over the radiator under the window. "It's not how I work. And it's not worth anything more than one two five." He lifted up her hand and pressed it against the towel to hold it up. "There's no point in lying to you," he said. "I know it doesn't touch the sides of what you owe, but upkeep hasn't been a priority and now it's letting you down."

Maggie felt her legs buckle. "Nothing?" she asked. "It really does nothing for you?"

Gandy brushed a few strands of her hair away from her eyes. She looked up at him. Mottle cheeked. Sodden eyed. Coils of hair matted across her forehead. She sniffed. "Really? That's all I'm worth?"

His reply was to never forget that there was still the word hope in hopeless.

*

After Gandy left, Jason bounded up the stairs two at a time to find his mother in a heap on the bedroom carpet, her blouse and bra wide open. She refused to look at him, just kept on wailing, and not even two stinging slaps across her face would make her stop.

"Did he do this?" Jason shouted. "Or did you?"

He raised his hand a third time, a fourth, perhaps a fifth. She was trying to tell him something through a bust lip – something about how that little man with his hammer should've put *her* out of her fucking misery, because who'd care, she was muttering, who gives a shit about me?

"What the fuck are you talking about?" Jason yelled. "What man with what hammer?"

And she told him that there was no point in pressing charges. Even the police had told her there was no point because it was nothing more than a mild threat with many conflicting viewpoints as some said they saw nothing at all.

She gave Jason his address anyway. Well, what she knew of it which was simply Bennett Road. And as she did, the penny dropped.

She knew she'd seen him somewhere before. But that was not something she was going to tell her son.

Round 17

Totty Minton was off his face with self-pity and a lack of sleep. He stepped out onto the stage at the far side of the school hall and took a deep, deep breath.

This was the fourth time he'd mounted this stage. The first was to accept a swimming badge, the second to blow down a recorder, the third because he'd been a member of Robin's merry men in the Christmas play; a bit part with one line he'd struggled to get out on time.

No-one else would remember those times. He hardly remembers them himself; cannot recall the distance he'd swum, the tune he'd played, the line he'd struggled to remember even then. But he wasn't going to forget this time. No-one would forget him this time because this time he'd got it all planned out. He would sing for their attention. He would tell them how it is. Then he would paint them a rainbow, perhaps even drown in its gold, and he stepped up onto his toolbox and began to give the performance of his life.

"Hey diddle, diddle,

We've been on the fiddle.

We thought we might live on the moon.

But none of us laughed, for it's not any fun,

When an overdraft that big goes boom…"

No-one looked.

No-one took a blind bit of notice.

"Three blind men, three blind men.

See how they run, see how they run.

They all went after the working wife,

And cut off the jobs from her husband's life,

Have you ever seen such a thing in your life,

As so many broke men, so many broken men…"

"Who organised the cabaret?" Jake nudged Della. "He's pissed out of his skull."

"I applaud anyone with the guts to get up there and have their say," Della replied, clapping her hands in Totty's direction. "It doesn't mean he's any more undeserving."

"You think nursery rhymes as manifesto *is* gutsy?" Jake mocked. "He's pond-life Della. Look at him! Men like him are why men like me have jobs like we do."

"And that's supposed to explain why you don't want anything to do with our child?"

Jake sighed heavily. It was a mistake to come here. He'd known from the moment he'd entered the school hall and found Della manning the desk, both hands on the ballot box, and swamped in a wildly printed Kaftan, not for its comfort but for its plum-tomato redness, and looking a little too moist around the eyes. She had voted huffily, feeling disappointed and betrayed by the only party she knew: "You see, I *am* a socialist because I believe in free health care and free education and I *am* a teacher for that very reason. But then to be told that I don't qualify for maternity pay," and she'd shaken her head at the elderly woman who was offering up her vote but very little sympathy for Della's predicament.

Earlier, Jake had approached Della with caution - they had not seen each other for over a month now, and though he'd listed the things he ought to say - she was blossoming, pregnancy really suited her, and it wasn't really about the money - she wasn't, it didn't, and it was.

"It was you who wanted in on the mortgage Della," Jake had reminded her. "And if I'm going to sell then you either need to update your share or we work out a deal that reflects your contributions."

Della had ignored him at first, instead looking at how the elderly woman had voted. "Another UKIP," she'd snarled, shoving the vote down into the ballot box. "People like her are so confused. They think the country's full of immigrants stealing our jobs and hustling our welfare system. It's a vote that screeches 'get the foreigners out'. But you can't be a democracy and then run a guest-list."

It was her usual self-righteous neurosis speaking; not quite thought-out and delivered in a flap, but Jake was more bothered for her actions rather than her words. He'd hissed, "I know you're angry and pregnant Della, but it's not any of your business what people vote."

"UK independence" she'd retorted. "What a joke. It'd be more appropriate if it were called the UK-*de*pendence party, for we're all dependent upon buying someone else's stuff rather than our own," and she'd asked Jake if he was now selling his goodwill and affection. "Seeing as you now speak of our relationship in pounds sterling. It's the only time I shall ever wish we'd joined the euro," and she'd shoved him aside so she could take another two voting slips off a couple stood to his left.

"Don't you dare," he'd said under his breath.

"The privileged few," she'd muttered, as she'd scrunched up their slips and shoved them into her own pocket. "Vote for the trees and you vote for the thorns, a bed-full of nettles. I can admire a meadow as much as anyone else, but I'd much rather admire the hospital ward I'm admiring the meadow from."

"And I'm asking you to stop doing that," Jake had sneered. "I'm sure it's against the law."

"So was Iraq. And Afghanistan. But we still went in looking for weapons that didn't exist," and she'd snatched the voting slips from the hands of another couple, only to shove them so hard into the ballot box that she gave herself a splinter.

"Look at the state of me," she'd said, fighting back tears. "This is professional poverty Jake. I'm barely surviving the month shopping for *our* baby on the never-never, and yet you're standing here asking me to up my mortgage contributions?"

He'd looked down at his feet and wished he'd worn older shoes. "You wanted in Della," he'd said glumly. "And now I just want out."

That, however, was as far as their conversation went, because Totty had then taken to the stage.

"Sing a song of sixpence, a penny for the guy.

Four and twenty Tories, playing I-Spy,

And when the dole door opens, they all begin to sing,

What we going to do with them, they don't earn a thing!

The kings are in their counting house counting all their money.

The queens are in their parlours, dripping with bread and honey.

The kids are in the gardens, their futures full of woes,

Cos daddy hasn't got a job since all the pot-banks closed!"

"Vote for you!" Totty hollered, his hands balled into fists and punching the air. "Spoil your papers! You've no-one to vote for. It's Blue Labour or Red Tory - two shades of the same shit and war criminals on both sides. Vote for you, because no God can truly forgive those who fuck up his land!"

"I didn't think people still stood on soapboxes," said Jake.

"They don't," said Della pointing towards the stage. "That's a toolbox. And he's more balls than you."

"Standing on a primary school stage singing nursery rhymes takes balls when you're four years old. He just hasn't grown up and thinks someone owes him a living," and Jake raised his voice and shouted towards the stage, "Get a job, benefit boy!"

Della told him to hush himself. "Until you know what's caused him to get up on that stage you are in no position to judge," she said. "You're not at work now Jake. Everyone has a circumstance."

"And he's like every other bloke I deal with round here. Make a fucking mess of it and then expect someone else to feel sorry enough to clean it up."

Della shook her head. "You're so out-of-touch Jake. You couldn't free a fly from a spider's web," and she stepped closer towards the stage to hear Totty better.

She was the only one.

She thought of Hattersley. Scargill. Tony Benn. Michael Foot.

She smiled up at Totty. He looked down on her.

"Can you see me?" he asked.

She nodded. And when he looked at her like he didn't believe her, she mouthed, *"I'm listening."*

So he told her he went to this school. "Remember me, 1973? Cross legged, Monday morning assembly, fourth row from the back winding chewing gum into Sally Benn's hair - no relation. My father was on strike. The teachers were going on strike. They'd cancelled the Christmas play to save electricity. Switch off Something, the Government urged. Save our darkening souls. There was no point thinking about the future. The future was cold. No coal to be burned. No pots to be fired. No point to be learned."

Della agreed.

"You're a teacher aren't you? I can tell. I'll also tell you this: all this education costing the earth and yet the earth is really hurt. We've dug it, probed it, mined it, fracked it for *money, money, money, it's not funny. It's a rich man's world.* You think earthquakes and tidal waves are natural? That's just the earth's way of reminding you who is boss. Remember when the landscape told you who you were, what you were meant for, what your life was all about? Remember when here was red and made of clay? But then someone said why's yours bigger than mine? Why have you got that and I haven't? Why don't you come over here where the sun shines in pound signs and the men and women work for pennies? And before we knew it we were robbing Peter to pay Paul to rob Peter to pay Paul until Peter's pockets were empty because Paul had handed it all over to the GPs who diagnosed Peter with depression. And we all know how much that costs the state when we're all on the sick."

Totty beckoned Della in closer. "What about you, duck? You got anything for me to do?"

Della lowered her head and backed away. "I'm sorry," she said quietly. "I guess I don't contribute after all."

She turned away, furious with herself. Jake had always said that her opinions were little more than condiments at the dinner-party she'd just made him endure. All rant and no march, he used to tease in the taxi on the way home. A lot of words and no deeds. And she'd say, "That's because you own the deeds rich-lad, and you won't put my name on that mortgage."

"Fine," he'd said. "I'll get mum to draw up a contract tomorrow.

Happy?"

"Happy."

Happy? *Happy?*

Her name on a mortgage had made her *happy*?

"Our Della's got a mortgage," her mother had beamed at the neighbours. "She's really gone up in the world."

But she wasn't happy being up there. The slog of the repayments. The endless insurance policies. A bill for this. A bill for that. Her name on every one. "Who are we paying?" she'd once asked Jake, when a student teacher and living way beyond her means. "I mean, who really is getting paid here Jake?" He'd mocked her, said, "It's called the economy Della." "No, it's not," she'd replied with gusto. "It's a trap. One great big snare set by the gentry to hobble us." Jake had just laughed at her. "It's called aspiration, Della," he'd said. "And you're very guilty of that too." "Then I shan't aspire anymore to become one of *them*," she'd said. "However tasty the food looks, however hungry I am. I will not be fooled."

But she was, as we all are.

Lost in her thoughts, Della hadn't noticed that behind her, Totty was raising his claw hammer. She hadn't seen him prise open a tin of paint. Didn't know that he was dunking in his hand and slapping it against his chest. She just heard him shout, "The uniformed hand on the uninformed man. Help me someone! Tell me where they're hiding! Someone find me a job!"

She turned just as he jumped off the toolbox, his claw hammer aloft, a doleful look upon his face. He dropped his hand back into the paint. He jumped off the stage. He brandished that hammer. His hand reached out to whomever was closest – a full handprint on a navy donkey jacket; his fingertips grasping at a floral blouse; a tight grip on a cardigan; a smear of paint across a football shirt – Totty grappled at anyone within reach, his hands dripping with the pinkest gloss he could find until eventually, he reached out and caught Della, branding her swell with his fullest handprint yet.

"Live now let the children pay later," he said grinning.

"What are you doing?" and Jake was aside of Della, an arm stretched protectively against her belly.

Totty turned away from them to dunk both his hands into the paint. He lifted them to his mouth. "I'm biting the hand that doesn't feed me," he told Jake, licking up the paint. And then down into the pot again, *dunk, gloop,* he lifted his hands up and, this time, put them around his own neck. "What am I doing?" he asked. "I'm killing myself. Isn't that what they want? Less of us living off them?" And he choked and he spluttered and retched up his paint - a slow, slew of that watered-down red - and onto the school hall floor.

Della moved closer towards him again. "Look, I know you're pissed off," she began. "I'm pissed off too. All this austerity shit? It's bullshit propaganda to keep the banks in charge and the poor in check. But put the hammer down. Please. You don't need to be pissed off with that."

"Then do you dare me?"

Jake stepped in front of Della. "I don't know what you're trying to do. But just don't do it, ok?"

It was feeble and Jake knew it. It did little more than have Totty chanting again. "Don't do it, don't do it. Don't tarnish me with the same brush as you." Until he suddenly started to cry as if it was something he'd forgotten how to do. "Why don't they look after us?" he asked Jake, the tears racing down his cheeks. "Other countries do their damnedest to save dying species. Why won't they look after us?" And then, as quick as he'd turned on the tears, he began to laugh - loudly, raucously, morbidly - and then to chant - "Never explain, never apologise, do what you have to do. Never explain, never apologise, just do what you have to do" - and he lifted up the paint tin with the claw of his hammer and swung.

What a shot! Jake ducked and there stood Della and their baby got socked in the face.

Round 18

Jake Povey and Della Knight had met on new year's eve - she insisted in 2003, he thought it was already 2004. It was a gaudy bar, loud, lewd, and serving very bad wine; a place both had long grown out of and wouldn't frequent if it wasn't for drunken persuasion by friends they barely saw anymore. He'd reached across her at the bar claiming he was next to be served. She told him if chivalry was dead then she'd buy the drinks because she'd been waiting a good ten minutes if not longer and fuck it, she'd said. I've been staring at all you night and I don't see a wedding ring and you're not here with a girl. She'd paid for the drinks and then after the drinks she'd hailed them a cab and long after the cab she'd left Jake, the next morning, with mascara all over his pillows. Two months later and she asked to move in.

Six years in her book, five in his. Now all over and over what? An argument he'd started with the words - *We should still consider our options.*

Last night, the man on the toolbox in the polling station was convinced he'd no options. At least, that was one way of looking at it; that he thought himself clean out of choice. But options were a social worker's currency and Jake had learnt to use them well: If we give you (a) then we're looking at (b) but (c) is not on the table unless we start considering (d) and that might be a little out of your league. It's still an option though. Not entirely out of reach. We'll talk about that next week if you get (e) done and are part way to showing me you can also do (f). *Off.*

Options.

In Jake's world there were plenty. Always an alternative. One over the other. Something always to decide. But really? You really want a baby?

"Yes Jake. I do."

It'd not been an option. Not in his book.

"Well that's that then." No option in Della's book either.

"We should still consider our options, Della."

"We? Who's *we* Jake? Who *is we*?"

Five months on and a man without options brought them together in circumstances that made a pain in his chest. Or was it his option to sell the flat and move on that'd brought them together? Wasn't that why he'd gone to see her? The man with the paint and no options was happenstance. *These things happen.* And Jake suddenly wondered what had happened to him: suddenly so unexplainably concerned for Della and the baby, he'd no other option but to drive her to the hospital himself - "Just to check. Put your mind at rest." So he'd no idea what'd happened to the man with the paint. There'd been a crowd around him and a crowd around Della, one crowd carrying the other away from the other crowd as if they'd been locked in a cockfight to the death. Nor could he remember anything that the man, that small, small man, had said when shouting from the stage. He'd been trying to make a point about something and resenting everything else.

But Jake remembered the paint and he remembered the hammer. The toolbox. The overalls. The way the paint had swung. The colour of it: a sort of washed-out red like peeled strawberries. Or yoghurt. Those sickly pink yoghurts that kids love. *Petit Filous*. Petit man and his even smaller point was nothing but a Petit Fool.

And so here he was: City General A&E. Never somewhere you ever wanted to be. White walls. Pot plants. Some real. Most not. TV's. Muted. Water fountain. A quarter full. Three cups left. Fairly comfy chairs. Green leather. Fake leather. They left red marks on bare legs. Vending machine to the left flashing, though there's a Starbucks to the right now, its grills pulled down, its last barista standing, mopping behind the counter and ignoring Jake's pleas to reopen.

He slumped back to the waiting area to wait some more. He's been here for almost three hours and it was nearing midnight. Seconds lasting minutes. Minutes lasting hours. No rush. Waiting.

Waiting. For news. Good news. It *needed* to be good news. Della had disappeared down a corridor in a wheelchair telling the porter above her, *It's not blood. It's dried pink paint. It was a tin of paint. Here. It got me here,* and she was yet to return. Jake closed his eyes and began to drift...

...Babies in Jake's book took bravery. Lifelong commitment. Things he now asked people to do. Like have dedication, show devotion. No. That's a song. A song he can't remember. Doesn't want to remember. *Turn that bloody music down!* It's his father. *I can't hear myself think!* A quiet house. Such a quiet house. He could hardly bear it. And he's what, fourteen, fifteen years old? His own bedroom. Lying on his bed. The only child. The spoilt brat. Gifts given because no-one listened. The vinyl this time is pink, neon pink. Pink like that paint. Records bought with paper round money. Records played and then turned off. *Turn that bloody racket off!* A quiet house. Such a quiet house. So quiet he could hardly bear it. Headphones. He remembers headphones one Christmas. Or birthday? Bought for his birthday. *From dad,* said the tag. He'd clamp on those headphones and turn up the volume. If they weren't listening then neither would he. Then he turns sixteen and sneaks a girl up the stairs. *Listen to this,* he'd said giving her his headphones. So she did.

Pink. She was so very pink.

Jake wasn't brave enough to have a baby. Not again. Dedication. Devotion. What the hell was that song? It'd cost him the earth in maintenance; demands for private this and privatised that, yet the daughter, *his daughter,* had not wanted to see him. Until she turned sixteen. Then she was at the door. *Mum was this and mum is that.* They started to hang out a little. He played her records without headphones and the volume turned up. *What's this? Can I have this pink one? What's it worth?* He'd clawed back time through his record collection, giving most of it away. *I didn't do anything wrong,* he would tell himself. *I only did what I thought was right.* Right for him. Wrong for everyone else. Pink. She was so very pink.

She's twenty-three now. Abi. Abigail Honey. Seven earrings in each ear and the tattoo of honey pot he'd paid for, she'd designed, somewhere on her body where a taste of honey could be found. Jake slumped deeper into his chair, deeper into his own mind. Dedication. Devotion. Realising that he was neither. Like father like son. What was that song? *We did something wrong.* No. *I did something wrong.* He pushed the palms of his hands into his eyes. Pink. She was so very pink. Make it go away. *Make them all go away.*

"You know, I say that every day but it never does."

Jake removed his hands and lifted his head.

"I ask myself all the time. Do I come here because I want it to stop or because I enjoy the company, the vending machine cups of tea?" and the woman raised her cup in Jake's direction. "I know you can't take your eyes off me," as Jake realised who she was. "I was a size 10 once. There was a time when even you would've fancied shagging me."

Jake shook his head at her. "You should never have let him come home, Maggie," he told her quietly as he clocked her black eye, bruised cheek, and bust lip. "What the hell have you let him do to you now?"

"I'm his mother," she reminded him. "And no mother gives up on their child, even when the state does."

"I did not give up."

"No," she said smiling. "My mistake. I gave him up. Because you said that way it would stop."

Jake Povey and Maggie Gifford: they'd not seen each other in a very long time though Jake had never forgotten her. He'd once kept tabs on Maggie's life as much as his curiosity thought necessary, but, truth be told, she'd been a head-case he'd been glad to handover to a woman expert in domestic violence. Other than hearing that Jason had done four months of an eight month stretch in a borstal, he had thought no more about them. Not because he could do things like that, but because he had to stop thinking about them. They'd almost ruined him. The insomnia alone had been so terrific he'd thought he was going mad.

He turned away from Maggie and looked up at the muted television set parked up on a shelf aside of a pot plant no-one watered. It was election night coverage. Local news fumbling about polling stations. He said to her, "If this doesn't make you have him up for GBH then at least go for harassment, alarm, and distress, Section 5 of the Public Order Act," and he even foraged in his pockets for a pen and paper to write it down. "Seriously Maggie," and this time he stole a quick glance at her face before his stomach turned over. "If you don't he will probably kill you."

Maggie burst out laughing. "Fucking social workers," and she shook her head at him. "We're all just door-knocking to you lot, aren't we? Knock and fucking run," and she watched the subtitles on the television screen for awhile.

"Free Enterprise. Freedom of choice. Rewards and self-improvement come with hard work. It's Cameron's natural instinct to want to reflect all that Thatcher did right for this country." A conservative majority expected in Battersea... Labour hold tight to Darlington and Durham North... "Hung parliament territory" Alan Johnson tells BBC... David Cameron on ConservativeHome says – "This is a decisive rejection of Labour. We can govern with this result."

Politics bored Maggie. She hadn't voted in ages. She had no reason to. No-one did anything for her. She worked. Felt guilty, came home. She paid in her taxes. National Insurance. Got nothing back. No assurances. No reassurances. Sometimes, she wanted to stand in the middle of the road like a bollard with a placard around her neck that simply said *Help*. Hoped that a driver wouldn't swerve to avoid her. Something had to make it all stop. She looked up at the TV screen and read the new scroll of subtitles.

The Conservatives hold Putney, 9.9% swing from Labour to the Conservatives... Sky News reporting 150-200 voters still waiting to vote in Sheffield... Police have been called to some polling stations to move on people who wanted to vote but couldn't because they were still queuing outside at 10pm. "The law states that the doors to polling stations must be closed at 10pm exactly, and no-one may be issued with a ballot paper after 10pm" a spokesperson says... Vince Cable says exit polls looking "very strange."

"Well, what do you know?" Maggie murmured at the telly. "They've actually found a way to close the bloody doors on us."

"You need to see someone Maggie," Jake told her. "You need to sober up and you need to see someone. There are places you can go."

"Good," she said. "Because I gave my house away tonight."

"Excuse me?"

"My house," she explained. "I gave it away. To Malcolm Gandy."

So that's why Jason had knocked her about.

"Jesus Maggie."

"I gave it away," she whispered. "Because how else will I make it all stop?"

"There were places you could've gone. You still could. I could help."

"Maybe I don't want to. Maybe I like it this way."

"And you've had no other male admittances at all this evening?"

Jake bolted upright in his seat.

"No-one at all?" and Constance Minton was indignant in black mackintosh and headscarf at the reception desk. "You're absolutely sure that no other man has set foot through those doors this evening? Please, check again. Minton, let me spell it for you. M-I-N-T-O-N, like the crockery, the factory, for crying out loud! Can't you hear me? Josiah Minton."

"Mrs Minton?"

Constance froze.

"My goodness, it is you. Is everything ok? Are you sick?"

Constance did not turn around at once. She had a smile to prepare, a situation to remedy, a reason to drum up in her head. She'd been out looking for most of the night. Old haunts, new locals, multi-storey car parks, and gravestones: Frank's mobile was peculiarly switched off. So was Totty's. But it was probably lost. She would get him a new one. Make a note of it on the calendar by the fridge and get him a posh one that took photographs and played tunes. Everyone letting her down. Her boys shutting her out. Her son planning to move to a bigger house she didn't know where. Frank saying what he said then *running* away from her, actually running: this was not how things worked. So when she eventually did turn about, when Jake saw what sections of her face she had not concealed by her headscarf, he could have well believed that she was actually here for herself.

"You don't look at all well," he said. "Is your son not with you?" He looked about.

Constance's mouth pursed. To the contrary, she explained, she and the family were quite well, thank you, and yes, of course the children were at home under their father's watch. "I was here to keep a friend company," Constance informed. "I was asking reception to book me a taxi home. I like to know what I'm getting into at this time of night."

"I can drive you home."

"I'd rather you didn't."

"It's midnight Mrs Minton, let me take you home."

"I rather think your pregnant wife would like to go home," her eyes gesturing towards Della who was standing by a pair of open double doors behind him.

It was uncanny how Constance managed to give him the slip in the time it took him to turn and look at Della then turn back to appeal to whatever common sense she had left. He swung back to face Della frustrated.

"Always was someone else you had to go and see," said Maggie, smirking up from her chair. "You haven't changed a bit Povey. Still finding crisis a turn on." She got up from her chair and looked down at Della's belly. "Girl or boy?" she asked.

Della, uncomfortable with the question and afraid to look at the woman's face, said she didn't know.

"I would," Maggie told her. "Just in case what you take home grows into something you don't want to go home to," and she staggered a little, flopping the upper-half of her body into Jake's chest. He grabbed hold of her elbows to steady her and she looked up into his eyes and saw the subtitles ticking past.

Battered mothers. Unfit wives. Lost fathers. Scavenging kids. New Labour. The New Middle-Class. The Public Sector. Dire Straits. Council houses. Welfare state. Laid to rest. RIP 1996-2010.

Jake looked over Maggie's head at the hospital doors. Dire straits. Of course! Over and over and louder and louder. *Dedication,* Maggie was yelling at him. *Devotion,* Della yelled from over there. *You really do get this all wrong.* Louder and louder and all in his head . Make it stop. MAKE IT STOP!

That's when it clicked. That's when he started to listen. The man on the toolbox was Constance's son.

Friday 7th May

2010

Round 19

Della's mother took her morning news with a pot of Earl Grey and a bowl of granola. Though she lived a sparse little life since being unexpectedly widowed at sixty-one, appearances had been fully dusted down and kept up including this, her new choice of newspaper which she had delivered by a young boy she could barely afford to pay.

"So I'm sorry Della," she said with a cocked-up little finger, her daughter despairing at the Telegraph's headline. "But Mr Clegg is only doing what any underdog would do when he spots an ajar backdoor. He goes in and puts the kettle on. Then waits for someone else to offer him tea."

"But why don't you care who makes the tea?" Della wailed. "Why didn't you vote? You're one of too many now mother, and that's why the bloody Tories have sidled in. It makes me sick to live with such apathy."

"Abstention is not apathy Della."

"You still didn't vote. And Roy bloody Dingwall got in!"

"No. I went to the school hall and told them I wanted to abstain from voting and so the lady gave me a lovely red felt tip to spoil my paper with. If I was apathetic I would've stayed at home."

"And pretty little pictures is just what Gordon Brown wants to see this morning," Della sniffed.

"You see, there you go again, assume, assume," and Mrs Knight poured herself a second cup of tea. "I wrote down some numbers actually. That there were 244,800 miners employed in the collieries here in 1984 and just three pits left today. That in 1958, there were 2,000 kilns in use, 298 factories, and seventy odd thousand pottery workers. Last year there were just 9,000 people employed in the factories, forty-seven kilns cold as the grave. That, Della, is not a pretty little picture," and Mrs Knight lit her third cigarette of the day and parked it up after a puff or two on her saucer.

Della coughed and waved her hands through the cigarette's smoke. "I'm *still* pregnant mother," she pointed out.

"Which is delightful news given what happened to you last night. And though I agree that man should be locked up, today is a new day dear. We must carry on and think of the baby. No more *stress*."

Della lowered her eyes and stroked her belly softly. "When I think of what could've happened."

"Well it didn't," said Mrs Knight quickly, nipping her daughter's wallowing in the bud. "And now you have to go to work."

Della sighed. "Yes," she said. "I have to go to bloody work."

"Why must you insist upon always thinking that things are so very difficult for you?" Della's eyes widened at her mother's cutting tone. "I had to work to keep you Della, and believe me, life is nowhere near as tough now as it was when I was pregnant with you." She picked up her cigarette and dragged on it with the sort of verve she saved for this, her third fag of the day and always her most enjoyed. "Sometimes, you lot really don't know you're born."

"And sometimes," began Della, waving away the smoke. "It's a wonder I ever was." She kissed her mother on her forehead and made to get ready for work.

"Oh by the way. A policeman came round last night," Mrs Knight suddenly remembered. "Came to see if you were ok. Nice man. Only lives round the corner yet I've never seen him before. Blatch his name was. Left a number. It's on the telephone pad." She gestured towards her small and pokey hallway. "It's what you need is a good policeman, Della. You know where you are with a man of the law and a woman in your condition wants that sort of security. Though I have to say, he was more concerned with what you were planning to do."

"Planning to do?" Della repeated.

"It's certainly something to think about," Mrs Knight replied. "You'll be out of work soon. State maternity pay. Single mother. You're surely not thinking of going back full-time because I'm no nanny dear." She looked up at her daughter. "It is an option Della. And Jake's mother is a solicitor. Don't presume that they'll side with the mother on this."

Della looked down at her belly again and closed her eyes. She remembered so little of what had happened last night. She remembered even less of him. The culprit. Her attacker. The man with the paint and no point.

"He was so very small," she murmured. "And so angry. So lost. You could see right through him." She opened her eyes, felt a small nudge from the baby inside and smiled. "You can't break what's already broken, mother. No point looking for compensation from someone like that. They've nothing to start with. What would I get? A pound a week?"

"Don't be a fool," said Mrs Knight, stubbing out her cigarette in the saucer. "Think about the boot being on the other foot before you make another one of your rash decisions. That type of person wouldn't be considering your state when filing *their* claim."

And then, just like that, Della realised whose boots had been stood on that toolbox last night: of just how little he had and how really small he was.

Round 20

Frank Blatch doused his face with warm Evian, reached for his Marlboros, lit one, smoked one, lit a second for the road. He wound down the window, felt a harsh wind blowing in from the right, saw a dark cloud brewing over the left. He'd voted with a heavy heart and a blunt pencil, backing the non-runner who was blind in one eye. He wondered what that was like, to have just one view, and he lifted his hand and placed it over his right eye.

In his blind spot, two posh blokes in smug suits and purple ties met on the wasteland to the right of Frank's car and shook hands. One had been re-elected into council and was yet to sleep. The other was reminding him of the fat donation that'd bankrolled his campaign, and successfully so. Both dug their hands into their trouser pockets and turned to look at what the wasteland faced. One carried on talking. The other listened and agreed. Both pointed at the house on the end. One said to the other, "They're still my houses. Bennett Road, it belongs to me."

"My advice is to be patient," the other said. "Your rents on headcount and zero-hours will be legitimised soon. You'll get what you want."

"Good," said the other. "Because my investors are ready to go."

"You'll get your little houses, Malcolm. No-one's forgotten you."

"Houses?" and Malcolm Gandy rattled spare change in his pocket along with car keys and aspirin. "You think I've pulled this lot down to put them back up again? This is the new precinct of bedsits, Roy. You signed off the plans yourself."

Councillor Roy Dingwall frowned. He remembered the original plans, the ones Malcolm Gandy on behalf of MG Estates had hand-delivered some four, five years ago now, and the spirited presentation they'd fallen for.

"Out of any ashes comes good compost for English roses. Dereliction is just the starting point. We won't build. We'll rebuild. We won't form. We'll reform. We won't invent the brick. We'll reinvent it. We guarantee there's a heart in every home we build."

But they were for houses, *affordable* houses - *Building your future a better future.* Roy didn't remember seeing any plans for a precinct of bedsits.

But it'd been a long night. He'd not slept. Barely eaten. The last thing that'd passed his lips had been a large brandy and a kiss from his wife before she'd retired for the evening at around 5am. As he would've done himself if he'd not taken Malcolm Gandy's call; his mobile beeping at 5.15am as he smoked on his patio and watched a new sun rise. Gandy had been very specific about them meeting and when.

Roy looked at the man and who's money had bought him election. He still couldn't quite believe it. It'd seemed such a long-shot when Gandy had proposed the idea. There was no way he'd get back in and certainly not when batting for the other side. But Gandy had just smiled. He knew that people round here would vote for the person and not the party. That people were more likely to tick the box aside of his name knowing, with a squint of concentration and their forefinger pressed hard under the letters, that despite his fallen reputation, Roy Edmond Dingwall still spelt **RED.**

And yet Edmond Roy Dingwall, as he had started out, appeared on the 20th February 1951 a lurid shade of yellow and some thirty seconds before the birth of James Gordon Brown.

Not that he knows this. He used to say it to cement his politics; politics that were inspired by a shabby undernourished childhood with neither bath nor hot running water and a father that beat the working class into him: he'd been a brute of a union man - hard-drinking, hard-talking, hard with women, who resented hard work and his hard time. He'd once divided the marital bedroom into two separate rooms - one still big enough to house the marital bedstead, and the other for a barrack that creaked and buckled with every turn

- because that way, he would harden up his son.

A bigot, a bigamist, a coward, and a cheat, Roy's father confessed to having a second family shortly after he'd fitted the curtain rail to divide up the room. And yet, he was actually in love with a third woman no-one knew anything about other than she was so dirt poor she wore his vests as scarves and picked coal from the railway tracks for a shilling a sack. Despite knowing this, Roy's mother continued to invite her husband into her bed until one morning, she roused her son and the pair of them left with just the clothes on their backs.

A woman from work took them in until the council provided a two-bed house to start again, just short of mile away from where they used to live. Luckily, Dingwall Snr didn't travel well, walked only to work, the pub and his woman, his *women*, and wouldn't be seen dead on a bus, so as it was, No. 1 Bennett Road ended up being terribly kind to Roy and his mother: despite the damp and the chilblains, the dirt, and the smells, and that he never brought a girl home out of embarrassment. (He'd even declined to buy the house from the council for £5,000 in 1985 because he didn't want his mother to know he'd got that sort of cash (and more) hanging about, or become known as someone who'd bought ex-council). His reputation was everything, even then.

He'd left Bennett Road shortly after turning eighteen. His mother asked him to go. Not because he'd insulted her, but because she'd been offered double his board and lodgings by a friend from work who was looking for a safe place for her daughter to bring up her baby. "Life's a business son," his mother's words. "And it keeps me off the streets."

Roy didn't argue. His mother had seen him right but would eventually go back to what she knew best which was giving men her best. So he caught the bus up to Keele where he found a room in student digs and earned a few business qualifications at night school. He went to his mother's every week for a Sunday roast and eventually married her lodger with the baby, cobbling enough money together to buy her a diamond the size of a pinprick.

The marriage faltered a decade back. They simply fell out of love. She moved to Leek to be closer to her mother. Their daughter (her baby) went to live down south. Their son (their child) worked in PR and had been the mastermind of Roy's political revival. Roy met his second wife on Friends Reunited. She used to sit behind him in maths and whisper the answers in his ear.

Roy only knew his father had died because he happened to be the next cremation after the funeral Roy had been attending. He laid no wreath and spat on his grave. His mother still lives but has, he hopes, put him from her mind, (as she has done with everything else that permanently confuses her) though he still visits her once a month for a Sunday roast and only when he gets up to leave does she remember, for a split-second, that he's her son.

Roy had not been in favour of the Bennett Road sale. At least not when he was last in office. But he'd a reputation to claw back, a career to rebuild: the papers had not been kind since he'd been caught with his pants down under the surgeon's knife in LA on expenses. Still, he'd done the decent thing and resigned, then publicly defected to the right where three years on, for old news was no news, he'd resubmitted his candidacy for council as a forgiven blue.

He had not expected to win office. No-one, not ever, voted blue in these parts. It was a ward with high unemployment, high crime, high anxieties, and high rises with a lack of high expectations, though the birth rate was particularly high and getting high was high on many people's daily agendas. It was, as most councillors agreed, a complacency not a constituency. But Roy had to restart his game somewhere and it was far better to get a head-start in campaigning to represent a ward that no other councillor wanted, or was ever likely to win. It was deep red in these parts. Blood red. Inbuilt in the soul. One generation to the next. Labour to the core. And no-one ever changed their minds or knew how to vote for anyone else.

But neither did Roy remember ever changing his mind about Bennett Road. Houses, yes. Affordable housing. That's what he remembers being presented. And he had agreed. Said, *Spruce the place up. Dust it down and give it a second shot.* Bennett Road had been kind to him. It was only fair to show it some kindness back. And as he glanced up he let his eyes run along what was left of the terraces he'd once known, and remembered as clear as day.

No.3 had all been loud speakers. Said what they thought and hid all they knew.

No.5 were called Cartwright. Washing would hang out on their line for days.

No.7 Roy couldn't really recall. Probably because the husband worked the night shift and the wife worked the day. Roy would watch them pass each other in the street:

(Him) *Morning duck, sun's out*

(Her) *Those sausages need eating and that shelf needs a new screw*

Their relationship grounded in the weather, home improvement, and out-of-date meat.

No.9 made their own Christmas cards, little grey sketches of the Smoke-on-Trent skyline, an area of outstanding natural beauty dipped in snow.

No.11 had wooden beads up at the windows and took in lodgers on the QT.

And No.13 were the Mintons. He vaguely remembers Constance. She must've been around thirty-five back then, thirty-six, maybe older, and he can see her now, face like a thunderclap, back and forth to work, hiding her poverty in starch and bleach and complaining bitterly about the weather, about the bus being late, about these new-fangled modern ways, *if only you knew how this really was for me*. But she lived like they all did. In endless drudge and loudly aired grievances in dark back kitchens about that drudge. He would walk past her many times and never once did he ever catch her eye.

He turned his thoughts to the brief meeting with Constance on her doorstep yesterday. Though so awkward it had made his arse twitch, she had not remembered him. Fifty years since they'd last clapped eyes on one another. Fifty years! The things he had done and seen, what he knew and had got away with in that time.

Fifty years!

And what had she done and seen? Where else had she been? She didn't know life without the house. The house didn't know a life without her. It was a life barely lived out. She asked for no other space in the world, and Roy looked down at his shoes and sighed. Thought then of his own mother sitting in a home with her mind back to front, her only complaint being that her girdle elastic was on its last legs.

"You know, they used to call them poorhouses, one family to a room, everyone grateful for what they'd got."

Gandy briefly acknowledged Roy's voice with a faint nod.

"Carnegie said 'there is no class so pitiably wretched as that which possesses money and nothing else'. I used to think that bullshit because when I was growing up right here, when we had fuck all, I thought money was everything." He rubbed an eye and looked back at the terraces. "What's another year or two?" he asked Gandy. "It's all she wants."

Gandy started to laugh. "I thought you'd bought yourself a new stomach," he jested. "Don't start having a fucking epiphany on me now."

Roy looked down at his feet. "Houses, *yes*. But bedsits?" and he paused, kicked at a ball of thick brown dirt at his feet. "If you could guarantee local employment perhaps?"

Gandy's face fell. "Do you have any idea for how many people are coming here without the skill-set to pay rent but are still ruled by an ingrained work ethic? After the campaign we've just led and you're now asking me to employ *local*?"

Roy continued to keep his head down. "Cream off a little workforce for the press release at least," he suggested.

"And it's a job in itself, councillor, to find them," and Gandy was irritated. "Half of them ain't fit. The other half work with their gobs. Then there's those that'll bang on about health and fucking safety for a shaving nick. I need to get going yesterday. It's a building site, Roy. Not a coalface."

"Then you've made your point," Roy told Gandy soberly. "And

that's why we're a democracy," and Roy held Gandy's glare for as long as he could stomach then backed away and retreated to his car, just as Frank Blatch removed his hand from his right eye and repeated the exercise with his left to see if there was any difference in the view.

Round 21

Constance fiddled with the dial on an old grease-spattered wireless she kept on the kitchen window sill. It found a signal. A woman's voice:

I voted Labour. Voting for anyone else is betraying your own sort...

Constance reached for the volume button and turned it up:

... Of course I voted UKIP. Most of my street voted UKIP. They just won't admit it. Stick a purple and yellow bunting up at yer window and you'll be bricked by morning. Posters like that are treason....

Constance shuffled over to the pantry in her slippers and counted her eggs. She took three, left one behind, returned to the stove and cracked each one gently into a pan, added milk, a twist of salt and pepper, started to stir. Scrambled eggs.

...The country is in absolute disarray. No-one's got enough votes to lead so they're all scrambling about trying to make friends like kids at a birthday party. And these men are supposed to be rulers?

Everyone wanting to make a deal. No-one making any decisions. Offers being made, offers declined: it seemed to Constance that the country was going backwards.

... There was no choice this time. None at all. And we don't have any choice in what happens now either. No, no, and no is how we all should've voted yesterday. Because not enough of us voted with children in mind...

Behind her, Joss and Kirty had slumped into chairs at the kitchen table. Joss poked his tongue out at his sister. She poked out hers in reply.

"Round nose," he goes.

"Big chin," she went. "What can I get you?" and she pressed two fingers against her lips and pretended to smoke, whilst Joss gave the matter some thought. Kirty clicked her fingers in his face. "Come on, come on. I haven't got all day duck. It's fast food is this and I'm a fast girl."

She was quoting from her mother, then a dismembered voice through a shining silver Tannoy system at the new McDonald's drive-thru three summers back. Everyone else had been. Everyone else had cars: Joss always mildly astonished by his sister's mind and what she plucked from it before his even kicked in.

Constance watched their role-play and wished the world were a better place. That people picked up their dog shit and didn't spit out their gum. That she could slip out of the backdoor knowing that even part-time parents were capable of full-time love, and Labour had got things right. *Really right.* Instead of thinking right to please the banks and woo the peers. She put three plates of scrambled egg on toast on the table with her usual brusque orders - roll up your cuffs, elbows away, no eating with your fingers - which made Kirty ask, "Has something bad happened to the world?"

"It's yet to wield its worst," Constance warned quickly. "But we'll just do what us lot always do. We'll grit our teeth and live through it," and she shook her head and sat down. "Do you remember what I told you to do when you're eighteen?"

Kirty dropped her knife and fork with a clatter and started to chant. "Don't get married, don't vote blue, go to university, don't get a baby due."

"Good girl," though Constance's eyes were locked on Joss. "I hope for your sake that you still remember that as well, young man."

Joss pointed his fork at his father's empty chair in reply. "Where is he?"

"He's working," as Constance tried to blank out the memory of how this little boy's face used to light up when his mother walked into the room.

Joss looked up at the kitchen clock. "He's at work? Now?" He snorted. "He's not even working is he?" and then, under his breath, "He doesn't know how."

Constance bit her lip and looked down at Totty's empty armchair, wondered if he'd been in a fight, if he'd been sick in the street, whether there was some slatternly girl with a dirty mind on the scene. "Mothers and sons have got to part," Ned used to tell her. "He's a man now Connie, and I'm *your* man," but she never could quite bring herself to agree. "I'd give up my own life if it meant extending his by another two foot," she was prone to say.

"You know, he does this every time she comes back," Joss interrupted her thoughts. "Her before us. Every time. So don't think she's not watching and seeing it all for herself, because she is. We all know she is. She's probably out there right now. With *him*."

Kirty's knife and fork clattered down on her plate again as she threw her arms over her head. "Can mum see me now? Is she watching us now?"

And there were tears. Crocodile, admittedly, but enough for Constance to lose her rag. "See what you've started?" sending a fork careering across the table, asking Joss if he felt proud. "Because this is your sister Joss, and you need to think before you speak. Or don't you have any feelings - like your mother?"

Joss jumped up from the kitchen table at this. "I feel a lot of things," he seethed. "But you taught me how to hide every single one," and he stormed from the kitchen and slammed the door.

Round 22

"Excuse me. It's Joss isn't it? Joss Minton? You're Kirty's brother."

"I'm getting the bus."

"I'm Della. Miss Knight. Kirty's teacher. Can I have a quick word?"

"You need to speak to my dad."

"No. It's erm... it's not like that. I'd rather speak to you if I can. I just wanted to ask you..."

"The bus. It doesn't really wait."

"Why is your mother always at the school gates?"

"What?"

"Isn't she allowed to see you?"

"Is that what she's telling you people?"

"I just thought..."

"A lot of you people do that about us."

"I'm Kirty's teacher Joss. I'm supposed to worry."

"You're pregnant. Worry about that."

"But if the school hasn't received any instructions..."

"We need instructions now?"

"It's upsetting your sister."

"She's not upset. Are you Kirt?"

"Nope."

"But you don't like it when you know she's there waiting?"

"I don't really mind it."

"That's not what you said last week, Kirty."

"I didn't like school last week. It was on my nerves."

"Look. I don't want to be rude but if I'm late, I'll get detention and if I get detention then I can't meet Kirty from school."

"Just one more minute Joss. Your dad. It's about your dad really. Is he, erm, like ok maybe, today?"

"What?"

"Your dad. Is he ok? I was just wondering if he was ok."

"My dad now."

"It's just that I've never met him and..."

"Want to guess who I am today, Miss Knight?"

"Not now Kirty. At parents' evenings, I mean. He doesn't come."

"He doesn't come to mine either."

"I bet you can't. I bet you three guesses that you can't guess who I am."

"Look. Dad is dad. Mum is mum. They are who they are and I've really got to go."

"But things are ok, at home I mean? Everything's ok? It's just that I think your father, erm, your dad, he was in the school last night and he was on the stage, with a toolbox..."

"Miss Knight! Guess what I am! Guess what I am right now!"

"I said not now Kirty!"

"Why can't you just be her teacher?"

"What? No! Joss, look. This is coming out all wrong. Last night, in the school hall, *this* school hall, your dad was on the stage and he had this toolbox..."

"But Miss Knight you're not ever going to know who I am if you don't play guessing right now."

"I've really got to get the bus."

"Miss Knight! Miss Knight!"

"OK, for goodness sake. What are you today, Kirty?"

"A mother hen."

"Are you? Well, look. Give me just one more minute, let me finish talking to your brother because this is important.... Joss, no I've not... Joss! I really need... Oh. Blow it."

"Do you know how chickens have to live Miss Knight?"

"What?"

"Did you know that they live in coops and have to keep laying eggs one after another and if they don't the cockerel orders his gang to peck their eyes out. Peck. Peck, Peck. And do you know why?"

"No. No Kirty. I don't."

"Because if you can't see where you have to live then it won't bother you where you have to lay your eggs, will it?"

"I.. what?"

"I bet you don't know the story about the woman who sat stroking a chicken either."

"I didn't know there was one."

"Well, there was this woman who was a cook but she was a cook who didn't like cooking animals. So she'd sit with them on her knee and be telling them that she was ever so sorry for cooking them, but she had to do it because she needed to feed her family. And the woman was crying because she didn't love her husband and had two babies that she didn't love either because they got on her nerves. And it was all because she loved this other cook and wanted to run away with him and take all the animals with them. So one day, both the cooks start to run. But they leave all the animals behind because that other cook doesn't want them after all and so all the animals bleat and stampede, but the woman who sat stroking the chicken doesn't even turn around and look back."

"That's...erm... that's quite some story Kirty."

"It isn't a story Miss Knight. It's real life."

"Right."

"And are you?"

"Am I what?"

"Right?"

"Well, yes, I am. But, no, I'm not right. God. I don't vote right. What? What are you asking me now?"

"Want to hear my three little pigs story now? It's got blood and guts and everything."

"I'm not sure we have the time now Kirty."

"You know how there was a little pig's house made of bricks? Well, after the wolf got drowned in the pot, the pigs ate him and then they got the builders in, the plasterers, and the decorators and if it wasn't the cement mixers getting on everyone's nerves it was the clod, clod, clod of work-boots going up and down the stairs. And then it was finished and they put up a For Sale sign and they said 'all offers considered.' And that's when the wolf's dad came to look at it in disguise. He said things like 'very nice' and 'I like the wallpaper' and then asked for another viewing and said he'd got loads of cash. And the pigs were like, yes, we've sold it! We can go and live somewhere where no wolves live! But when he came back the mother pig smelt his love of pig-blood straightaway. So she screamed blue murder for her piglets to run and they did. And they had to keep on running and running for all of their lives because there's nowhere in the world that wolves don't live. Ooooh the bell! Come on Miss Knight. We'll be late!"

"Shit. Shit. *Shit.*"

Round 23

Lux Faithful was not at all what Jake had expected. They were sat across from one another in a frostbitten room, the air conditioning on the blink, and the blinds pulled down. She was the type you'd spot instantly in a packed darkened room and gravitate towards in the hope of spending the night with her. Her packet-blonde hair was feathered into her neck, the style shaping her face and bringing out the colour of her eyes. They were her most prominent feature and expressed everything she felt. "They'll be the death of me in the end," she told Jake. And that when it came to Totty, "He's just never been allowed to grow into his adult skin."

Totty was still to arrive. Jake checked his watch and Lux told him not to bother. He wasn't coming. He doesn't understand what it is he's doing wrong. "And he doesn't tell the time either," she added. "Just gets stuck in it." She then told Jake that she'd had a jealous mother and a combative father, a combination that'd advised her to step on toes, roll heads, stab backs, crush dreams, throb hearts, sell souls, break legs, twist arms – "Growing up was bloody hard work," she assured Jake. "I was positively diddled out of my childhood."

When she became breathless with a story about how she was frequently left out in the rain whilst her parents went out drinking, she looked at the floor and explained that her mother used to accuse her of hypochondria as a child – "When it was panic Mr Povey, genuine panic that one day, my parents would forget me completely." She followed this with a story about a near-stabbing in her early twenties which made her fully conscious of life's brevity. "It could've gone either way," she said dramatically. "That knife positively gleamed life's choices at me, so you could say it's why I live a life how I want."

Jake checked the time again. They'd been talking for half an hour. He'd spent most of that time doodling spirals and lightning bolts in the margins of his notepad and he needed to take a break. He felt drained by her, enchanted by her, and he could do little else but excuse himself from her company before it really did start to feel like a date.

He headed off into the communal kitchen, spent a couple of minutes checking for chips and hairline cracks on the mugs, then steeped two teabags in hot water from the urn, added milk, but had forgotten to ask if she took sugar.

"So what kind of bullshit did Totty Minton conjure up this time for not turning up?" and Ursula flashed her wristwatch in his face. "That says a quarter past ten," she mocked. "That's a big fuck-you by my reckoning," and Jake's forehead slumped onto the cupboard in front of him.

"I met him last night," he murmured, as Ursula removed the teabags from the two mugs. "Totty Minton. He was there. In the school hall. Voting."

"I hear he put on quite the cabaret," slopping the teabags into the bin. "Small town, big mouths, narrow minds," she said. "How's Della? I hear she took quite a swing of paint."

Jake glared. "She's fine." He picked up the two mugs and turned to make his way back to Lux.

"Congratulations by the way," Ursula called after him. "You should've said you were going to be a dad. Explains why you've been so distracted."

But Jake didn't turn around. He put both mugs of tea on the desk and sat down with a straight back. "We need to start this as we mean to go on," he began. "I represent the children Ms Faithful. *Your* children. Do you understand?"

"Oh yes," she agreed, as her perfume caught the back of his throat.

"I know Mr Minton isn't here right now, but you haven't been here for almost three years."

"And your point is?"

"Consider your own inconsistencies before you continue with these unfounded insinuations," and it'd come out exactly as he had wanted it to sound.

Lux rose up from the chair and stepped towards him to cup his chin. "Hmmm," she murmured, as Jake flinched at her touch but mindful that he could not and must not touch her in any way. "I thought so. You don't look like a father. Not at all. And you certainly don't want to be one." She released his chin with a stroke of her fingers and protruded her own in his direction. "In cases of divorce Mr Povey, children become a matter of allocation. If Totty and I *had* married then we would divorce and time-share our children, but because we're not married, my leaving is considered as straightforward abandonment which gives me no rights. And yet I'm their mother. How is that fair?"

"Ms Faithful. If you could please take your seat."

"I'm playing this by the book Mr Povey," she interrupted. "Your way, your rules, no contact unless under official supervision, though I expect he didn't make the appointment yesterday either," and she started to smile. "I thought not. Perhaps now you might understand how hard it is to love a man who won't love his children enough to learn to read them a bedtime story," and she sighed hard as she finally returned to her chair.

"It's why I've appointed solicitors. I'm genuinely concerned for both how and where they sleep, including my son's extra-curricular sleeping arrangements," and she paused to ensure that Jake had heard her correct. "He's fifteen Mr Povey. He's still a child. And though I'm no stranger to curiosity, it's also illegal and that makes it a matter of neglect upon the supervising parent's part." And she paused again, wondering if she needed to cement her point further. She did anyway.

"They're both so wrapped up in *their* needs and *this* eviction - which I assure you, Mr Povey, Malcolm Gandy has done his utmost and more to help with - that they've absolutely no idea what Joss is doing half the time. I mean, do you? You've been asked to monitor my family Mr Povey, and I bet you've no idea where he's been these past two days whilst his father goes up the wall again. Did you know that?" And she beckoned Jake to come closer. She placed her hand on his shoulder and whispered into his ear. "My son is dipping his wick Mr Povey, and what scares me is where that curiosity goes next. What happens then? Is that what it's going to take? Another little Minton?" and she decided it was probably for the best to leave it at that and pulled away.

*

Ursula approached Jake's desk and tossed a pale blue folder at him. "You'll be going round there for Christmas fucking dinner next," her tone so sharp it could cut glass. "That is an incomplete assessment Povey and you know it."

Jake looked down at the file and at the word Minton scrawled across it in permanent marker. "We've seen far worse and not taken action," he said. "And those camp-beds are not half as disturbing as the malicious insinuations mum has just made because she can't get her own way."

Ursula pushed an alp of files aside and perched on the end of Jake's desk. "When are you going to get it into your thick head that the whole situation is disturbed?" she asked. "Dickhead-dad got chucked in the cells last night for paddling in pink paint in the school hall," she started to laugh. "He also spent most of Wednesday threatening some woman with a hammer in the Jobcentre because she wouldn't process his claim," and she unpicked a ball of Blu-tack off Jake's computer and began squeezing it between her fingers.

"Three years Lux Faithful has been absent from her children's lives and this shouldn't be about taking sides," Jake reminded her.

"Then get back round that house and make a proper fucking assessment like you're paid and trained to do," she said. "And then call Housing and find out whether that council purchase order has been sent to Constance. Not an eviction notice Povey. A council purchase order. Because this is not a department who condones kids who squat," and she pressed the Blu-tack back onto his computer with her thumb and headed back to her office.

Round 24

1st July. Potters' fortnight. 1978. Constance was frying four rashers of bacon when Malcolm Gandy called for Totty with a football under his arm. She'd turned away from the frying pan to tell the then twelve year old Totty that he must take a coat if he was going for a kick-about with Mally because it looked like rain.

Totty had run upstairs to his bedroom to find his cagoule which he only ever wore tied about his waist. Gandy had waited for him at the kitchen table - then a scabby-kneed hard-nut, his face sculpted by a father far too nifty with his fists. Constance had shuffled over and slipped him two ten pence pieces. "You'll get yourself some sweets, won't you son?" then put a finger to her lips and told him "Shhh," because Elsa said all those sweets would rot his teeth.

And so that afternoon, four twelve year old boys stood in Hunt's sweet shop pooling their money.

It'd been Hunt's sweet shop since 1959. It was still stuck in its time warp come potters' fortnight, 1978. Old scales on the counter, jars of hard toffees, gobstoppers, gumdrops, pear drops, and aniseed balls put high upon the shelves and out of harm's way, and he'd stand on a milk crate would Hunt behind the till; white lab coat, gold rimmed specs, stunted he was, polio they were told, but kids are mean and they took advantage. So when Hunt stepped off his milk crate to step onto his wooden ladder to reach the jar of gobstoppers, Gandy had seen that he was midway through a till count.

"It's no good wanting what you don't really need," was life according to Constance Minton. But three gobstoppers and a stick of gum was never enough for a boy like Malcolm Gandy who hadn't been brought up to share. *How much for a Pear Drop Mister? How much for the lot?*

It's why Gandy has always held Constance responsible. She gave him two ten pence pieces that day. He should've just pocketed them, spent them how *he* wanted. But she went and said to Totty, when he'd returned with his cagoule tied about his waist, "I've given Mally twenty pence for sweets. Don't leave anyone out now. Get Pear Drops or something that lasts." And that's how it'd begun.

Though it could've happened anywhere really; they could've been in any sweet shop on any street in any town in any country in the world. *Run all the way and don't stop until you get there.* The brown dirty Trent and that grey stick of gum. *Fish me out! I can't swim! Fish me out!* Floor sweepings, potato peelings, years of dust, sweat, and blood: he'd swallowed them all and grew heavy. It could've happened anywhere. It shouldn't really have happened at all. But it did. It'll all come out in the wash, they said, and Totty won't ever let Gandy forget it.

"Perhaps there really does come a time when you have to stop feeling resentful of everything that never happened," Constance often told her son.

And Totty would remind her, "But you weren't there."

"I didn't need to be," Constance would retaliate. "But I know that Gandy's frightened to death that you're right; that he did push Jonty into the canal."

"He did," Totty would insist.

"Then you should've spoken up back then," Constance would say. "Because that's not the same water in that canal anymore, and Malcolm Gandy is not the same boy."

Back then was when they were comrades. Totty Minton. Malcolm Gandy. Frank Blatch. Jonty Moffatt. *You'll never need a blade with a comrade* was their motto, because like clay, coal, and canals, one always needed the other. And to watch your back if you were pointing in the wrong direction. *We're all in this together.* Sucking on a Pear Drop until a translucent splinter was left on their tongues. And now?

"You hound the poor when it's us poor what made you, Malcolm Gandy," Constance berated on a regular basis.

To which Gandy would reply with a smug smirk, "The difference between men like me and men like Jonty is that one sinks and one comes up smelling of roses."

"You chucked a rock at his head."

"Connie, that's a filthy rumour I'd ask you not to spread."

*

It was terrifically humiliating to have been found by Gandy some thirty-two years later, stooped in the pantry, left breast clutched, breath heavy, right hand fumbling under her blouse checking for more lumps: Constance had been rearranging her tins into alphabetical order - *Baked beans, butter beans, carrots, peas, runner beans and sweetcorn, chopped tomatoes, plum tomatoes* – and "Dear God," she'd cried out just as Gandy pushed open the pantry door - rearranging the tins to distract from the pain that seared from her insides.

"This stops now, Connie," said Gandy, filling up her pantry doorway. He kept his hand on her shoulder, her skin like barbed wire underneath her blouse. She looked up at her pantry shelves, switched two tins of tomatoes around and told him that once a rationer never the most rational, and that some of these tins were out-of-date.

She came out of the pantry to make tea. She'd no cake and had not yet made the beds so the camp-beds remained in the parlour in her way. She filled the kettle. Clucked about biscuits. *I normally have custard creams.* Reapplied face powder by catching her reflection in the hot and cold water taps.

"What are you doing here Malcontent?"

He'd not heard that pet name in a long time.

"Astonishing how long you've survived without central heating," Gandy replied. "This place is as cold as the grave."

She smiled and told him cold hands, warm heart. "You must remember my lovely pastry if not your manners," referring to the way he'd poured his own tea first. "Always so self-involved, Malcolm," puckering up for a fight. "Am I to take it that you're here because I'm all on my own?"

"I've given him a house," Gandy declared, now pouring out her tea. "Place called Fairview, just short of the Carroway. Three bedrooms, nice little garden, proper driveway, needs a bit of work, but we'll call it rent. It's a big, open, comprehensive offer, all above board. I want you to tell him to take it."

"Well, I shan't," passing him the milk.

"It was always going to happen, Connie," Gandy replied. "Councils are strapped for cash. They can't afford the upkeep and I offered a cash sale. Anyone could've bought them. Isn't it better that it's me?"

"But it's always you and only ever you," Constance reminded him. "We can't get away from you."

"And you're not very well," he replied. "Are you?"

Constance looked away and placed a hand on her forehead. It was true that she wasn't particularly well today and she was tired. So very tired of it all. She had spent most of the morning wondering what it'd all been for and why she'd been no good at any of it. But then she'd snapped herself out of it and got on with her day. Gone to the pantry, for what, she no longer remembers.

"You can't protect him from your death as well Connie," Gandy was saying to her. "Try as you will. It's something you just cannot do."

He watched her scrunch up her hands in the pockets of her apron and for all the world he wanted to reach out and grab hold of one of those hands, hold it as tight as he could. But he did not. She would've mistaken the gesture for affection.

"He so looks up to you, Malcolm. Even now, after all you've done."

Gandy sighed and picked at a fingernail. "I'm giving him a house Connie, as I have offered you many."

"I can tell him everything you know. It won't matter a jot to me."

Another heaving sigh from Gandy. "Jonty Moffatt was hardly

going to set the world alight," he told her. "He couldn't have cared less whether he was pushed or not." He pulled out a set of keys from his jacket pocket and slat them down on the kitchen table. "You tell him to take it," he ordered. "Think of those children."

"My whole life is my children!"

"Then let them *all* grow up." He pointed at the keys again. "I'll send the best to move you all in. Unless you want that bungalow up Smallthorne, of course. It's still vacant."

"Get out," and she picked up the keys and threw them at his back as he made his way to the door.

Round 25

"So," said Jake, his notepad on his lap in the parlour of 13 Bennett Road. "Do you mind sleeping on a camp-bed?"

"No," said Kirty as she sat cross-legged on the hearth rug at Jake's feet. She was wearing her granddad's dusty old trilby, his reading glasses with the lenses pushed out, and with her own notepad at the ready, she chewed on her pen, and screwed up her nose.

"You know it's not a proper bed like other girls and boys have?" Jake continued.

Kirty pulled out her magnifying glass from the pocket of her jeans and looked up at Jake through it. "When we went exploring in Africa," she told him. "The African weather was so hot we had to sleep outside in the dirt because it was cooler and there was more room. And then when we went to India, we all slept on the floor on cardboard in the same room we ate in *and* bathed in every night."

"Yes, but you live in England," as she leant forward to inspect the soles of Jake's shoes with a knitting needle, because that was what hunters did when looking for tracks. "And you've never really lived anywhere, Kirty, but this house."

"But that's just the thing," she said, flicking a pebble out of his shoe grips. "Everyone keeps telling us that we need a house, but we've got one of those *and* we've got a home, so why don't you just give the house to someone who really needs it like the children in Africa?" and she picked up the pebble from the carpet and studied it through the magnifying glass. "Hmmm..." she said. "Very, *very* stony."

Jake scratched his nails across his forehead. "Kirty," he began. "You're avoiding my questions."

"You do know that all hunters sleep on camp-beds in their tents," she said. "You do know that all the men who went to war slept on camp-beds too? That makes them the beds of heroes."

Jake closed his eyes.

"And did you know that there are five pages of camp-beds in the Argos catalogue? Some are luxury. Some of them are a hundred pounds."

"Kirty."

"Daddy says that when the time comes when we have to live in oxygen tents and pay for the air in the sky to breathe, sales of camp-beds will soar."

"Is that right?"

"People will have shares in them."

"I see."

"Do you know why all hunters live in tents and sleep on camp-beds?" and she was still squinting through the glass at the pebble from Jake's shoe. Jake shook his head and told her no. "So they can keep on *being* hunters, silly," she said. "Because if they lived in the same place for all the time their prey would find out where they lived and then come hunting for them and kill them all in their sleep." And she made slicing sounds as she judo-chopped her hand this way and that way across Jake's shins.

*

The first piece of advice that Jake ever received from Ursula Rawson-Sage was that no theory, however sparkling, could stand up against gut instinct.

"That, and first-hand experience of having nothing," she'd told him, knowing that Jake was from very-well-to-do stock. She could tell by the way he wore his hair slightly parted, the backpacker's tattoos he tried to hide under his shirt sleeves: the way he answered the phone in a sing-song voice, ever so patient and dead calm. "Because people who've got nothing either don't want you to know that they've got nothing, or want to show you that they've had nothing," she'd explained. "We live not on our means but by what our stuff means, so I guarantee that what you'd call nothing, or consider as being hard-up, doesn't even touch the sides of what these people don't have."

Jake had dismissed Ursula's advice as the sort of womanly twaddle his own mother might spout when feeling taken for granted and having sunk one too many melancholies on ice. He'd seen true poverty on his gap-year travels of Asia, where he'd lain in hammocks kissing the toes of Kiwi backpackers with breasts like eggcups and beads in their hair and teaching the odd English class on the outskirts of Bangkok. He'd told Ursula, rather innocently, "We're not Third World poor though, not like that," and she'd hooted with laughter in reply.

"Oh God," she'd said. "Another middle class do-gooder who thinks he's helping out the world's poor. You're going to get the shock of your life."

She was right. Because sat crossed-legged on the floor playing hunters wasn't poverty, neglect, or deprivation. Most of the time, and especially now, Jake didn't know what to call it at all.

"Of course," said Kirty, her magnifying glass now *psychic-analysing* the threads in the turn-ups of Jake's trousers. "You know that's the answer I have to tell you."

Jake's eyebrows dropped. "What answer's that then, Kirty?"

"The answer about the camp-beds," she said, pointing at the two beds parked up against the sideboard behind her.

"What about the answer you shouldn't tell me?" he asked.

Kirty shifted onto the rug and pulled her knees up to her chest. "Well," she said stiffly, "sometimes my feet get really cold," and she asked if she could go to toilet before she burst.

*

Joss Minton sniffed the air as soon as he walked into the room.

"Don't do that," said Jake.

"But it's all bullshit," Joss told him. "You, dad, mum, round here..."

"And you've been here too many times for me to bullshit you," Jake interrupted him. "It's my job to ask questions, whatever I might think of the situation."

"It's a fucking joke that you get paid to tell us what to do," Joss snapped.

"I'm not telling you to do anything," Jake replied. "But you're better than this. You're different."

"No I'm not," and Joss slumped down into the settee cushions. "I'm no different to anyone else round here, and I'll tell you why. Because all I have to do is look at my dad and see that's all I've got to look forward to."

Jake put his pen down. "Are you aware of how that sounds?"

Joss shrugged. "I have children for parents, how else do you want me to say it?" He rubbed hard at his nose and sniffed. "But it's not really any of my business. And I don't think it's any of yours."

The words were well-practised. Joss had said them countless times before. He was wise to the process but careful not to outsmart it; to always remain fifteen years old.

"You get a mum and a dad and some people like theirs and lots of others don't," he pressed on. "So this is us. It's the way things are and they're as good as they're ever going to get. Mum sticks around when she wants to. Dad sticks around because he has to. Their problems are each other and they know exactly what they're doing."

"And as grown up as that sounds, don't you mind?" Jake asked.

"It's better than most get," Joss said. "Some parents have you then fuck off for good."

"And you think that's ok?"

"Once you can sleep on a camp-bed you can pretty much sleep anywhere."

"It really doesn't bother you for what your mum has been saying about you?"

Joss shrugged again. "Everyone says stuff they don't mean. And she knows it's not true anyway."

"So how old is your girlfriend?"

"I don't have a girlfriend."

"Your mum seems to think that you do and she's perhaps younger than you."

"Then you tell her from me to stop following me," and he jumped off the settee.

"Think about what it is that you're doing Joss," Jake said quickly. "You're just giving your mum more ammunition to get at your dad and get hold of you. You do get that, don't you?"

"I get a lot more than everybody thinks," he said. "And I don't have a girlfriend."

Jake followed Joss across the room. "You know that your biggest problem here is not those camp-beds but your girlfriend's bed. And somehow, your mum's got wind of it. She's making insinuations that could damage all of your lives," and he pushed his hands deep into his trouser pockets.

"I don't have a girlfriend," Joss repeated.

"And I know that I'm an arse with women," Jake confessed. "I have that on very good authority. But you're a whole lot cleverer than I was, and you don't deserve to have your life finished with a premature kid before it has even got started." He bent down for his notepad and snapped it shut. "Just be careful," he said. "Be aware."

"And I don't have a fucking girlfriend," and this time Joss raised his voice.

"Well, your mum's seen you with someone and put two and two together," Jake replied. "I'm just hoping that whatever she's seen doesn't make three," and he headed out of the room.

*

Constance was standing aside of her ironing board waiting for her iron to heat up when Jake re-entered the kitchen to collect his belongings. She sipped at a cup of tea and adjusted her reading glasses before taking a school-shirt out of her ironing basket and shaking it out.

"How is Mr Minton?" Jake asked her. "Was he ok after what happened last night?"

Constance shook the shirt a second time. "Last night, Mr Povey?"

"Accident and Emergency. Was all ok?"

Constance pulled the shirt across the ironing board and began to press the collars. "I'm sorry Mr Povey. I don't know what you're talking about."

"Last night, at the hospital," Jake repeated. "It was you, Mrs Minton. We even had a conversation."

Constance looked blank. "I'm ever so sorry Mr Povey," affable, unflappable. "But we all had an early night." And she looked him straight in the eye as if she truly had no idea for what he was talking about. She asked, "Anything else before you go? Please don't let us keep you from your wife and family."

"Why doesn't Mr Minton sleep in his room?" and even Jake was shocked for how quickly the words had dropped from his mouth.

"A working mind should never lie down," she retorted quickly. "Or do they not teach you that at private school?"

"You have two children sleeping on camp-beds in your front room and a bedroom upstairs not used."

Constance pressed the iron down hard on the shirt cuffs. "They said that Maggie paid for her own ironing board in Downing Street,"

141

she began. "That she'd happily spend an hour or so picking the fluff out of her tumble dryer. Yet she invented greed like no other, Mr Povey. She made us want tumble dryers then she made us want to employ someone to pick the fluff out of it in case we got our hands dirty." She turned the shirt over to address the sleeves. "Did you vote yesterday?"

"All politicians are as bad as each other," he said.

"That shouldn't stop you Mr Povey. Men like you. You have a choice," and she paused to smile. "Of course, don't come running to me when the cuts go deep. You might only have yourself to worry about but then you've only got yourself to blame if you couldn't be bothered to tick a box," and she winced, and then heaved, and Jake found his hand was reaching out to her.

"Mrs Minton?"

"Then again, when you cripple the fathers, you cripple the children. They've nobody to look up to anymore," and at that, her smile faded. "Of course, they're moving tomorrow, Totty and the kids. A three-bed house, just like you lot have wanted, so maybe we can finally just get on with our lives," and she finished the shirt and headed off into her pantry for coat-hangers.

"I'm sorry," he said. "But what three-bed house?"

"The one they're moving into tomorrow," she said. "Didn't I tell you?"

"No. It wasn't mentioned at all." He came towards her again. "Mrs Minton. This sort of information matters."

"But if it doesn't matter to us Mr Povey, then it shouldn't matter to you," and she bent down towards the ironing basket and lifted out a pair of Totty's overalls.

"I'm sorry," Jake said again. "But three-bed houses don't just fall out of the sky."

"What does it matter where the house came from?" she asked, stretching the overalls across the ironing board. "It was offered to them, they're moving into it and that should be the end of it. I do wonder if anyone is thinking about you whilst you do all this thinking about us," and she picked up the iron and flicked its switch to full steam. "Though I do promise you, Mr Povey, nobody *is* thinking about you. They're only thinking about themselves."

Jake ran a hand through his hair in frustration. "And does this house have an address?" he asked.

"Oh yes," said Constance, now wearing her best smile. "It's exactly where you want them," and she turned her back on him and began to iron a pair of overalls that her son hadn't worn in a decade.

Round 26

There were no charges. Just a caution.

"Bail?"

"Paid, mate."

"How much was I worth?"

"Someone thinks you're worth it."

"My toolbox?"

"At reception."

"Anyone waiting for me?"

"Nope."

Three flights of stairs to get there. Two corridors. Nothing on the walls. Fluorescents overhead. Four sets of double doors, and Totty was back where he'd started. He smelt over-percolated coffee. Bleach. And Pear Drops. Sucked on Pear Drops. *Mine's better than yours. Mine lasted longer.* Totty always the first to buckle and crunch.

He went to the reception desk to collect his belongings. They filled a single plastic bag. A key. Whatever pence he carried. A lighter. A roll-up. Chewing gum. A dog-eared Polaroid of a crumpled brother and sister sat on the swings up Hanley park. He didn't remember being brought in here. Didn't remember anyone searching his pockets. Just that he'd woken up having slept like a log.

He asked the non-descript copper behind the desk what the election results had been. "How we doing, mate?" was how he asked.

"Door's on the snip," the copper said. "All just wiping their feet on the Gordon Brown doormat waiting to go in."

"And me?" Totty asked. "Was I on the news?"

The non-descript copper sniffed. "Only proper murder makes the news lad. Spot of war. Boobs."

Totty scratched at his head. "Really?" he said. "Not even in the rag?" He pointed at the local newspaper the copper had rested his mug of coffee on. The response was a quick shrug and then head back down towards his paperwork.

Thump. Clunk. Clatter!

Totty's toolbox was dropped on the floor aside of him just shy of his feet. "Jesus!" He jumped out of the way.

"That needs two fucking hands not one and a half."

It was Frank. He chucked the chain that Totty had been using as a manacle and watched it slither to the floor with a tinny rattle. "That's what this circus of yours is all about? Getting in the fucking chip paper?"

Totty looked at him briefly and then turned back to the plastic bag of his belongings. He prised apart the seal and began stuffing the contents into his pockets.

"Why don't you ask me where I've been, comrade?" Frank again, hands now thrust deep into his uniform pockets.

Totty exhaled loudly. "Tenerife?"

"Shall we start with B&Q?" He pulled out a hand to count on his fingers. "I told him you were desperate and couldn't afford to lose the work. Said you didn't want your gaffer knowing you couldn't read shit and you'd panicked. Shall we talk about the school hall next? The pregnant teacher you smacked in the stomach?"

Now Totty turned about. "She must be ok," he said slowly. "They would've charged us otherwise." Frank grabbed him by the collar of his overalls and threw him against the wall.

"You're a harbinger of all that's gone bloody wrong round here.

You're a fucking liability, not a mate, and you've just gone one step too far with this fucking circus of yours." He pushed him hard against the wall and held him by the throat. "Why don't you do us all a favour and fuck off away from here, leave us all be?"

"And your fat feet have been under my mother's table since you were a nipper," Totty's eyes now bulging with rage. "You'll never replace me, comrade. She's not yours to have and neither are they."

Frank let him go at this and Totty dropped to the floor. He put a hand to his neck and coughed a little, his eyes fixed to a stain on the linoleum floor. He ran another hand through his hair, to his nose, over his eyes, his mouth, back through his hair, all the while his eyes fixed on the tiny splash of blood on the station's reception floor that might've been his, could easily have been someone else's, what did it matter? He was and well truly bled dry.

Round 27

Thrift and hard work, went the theory, the working man should be entitled to buy his own home. It'll make you a better citizen, provide stability for your family, be something to leave your kids when you're done. As Michael Heseltine said, "Home ownership stimulates the attitudes of independence and self-reliance that are the bedrock of a free society." Or something along those lines. And then, said Maggie, the market will build the houses. The council has better things to do. Other fish to fry. It's your right to buy. And three-bed houses, it seemed, fell out of the sky.

Though there was no record of this on the computer. Jake searched whatever category and file he could think of. "A three-bed house, just like you lot have wanted," was what Constance had said. The address? "Exactly where you want them."

He was distracted by a second beeping of a mobile phone receiving text messages that wasn't his. There was no-one else at work. Not at this time. Friday night, 7.30pm. Homes to go to, lives to live. Jake had driven away from 13 Bennett Road, confused. They were moving, Constance said, and tomorrow. Moving where? A house from where? He'd driven back to work to check on the system. Maybe someone had inputted data whilst he'd been on the visit. Maybe the house was there all along and he'd just missed it on the files. Can't see the wood for the trees where the old man hung and swayed in the breeze until he was found by a young copper off duty and walking his dog. He'd found that on the computer via a quick search on Google.

The mobile phone had now started to ring like the old fashioned dial-phone. *Brrrring, brrring. Brrring, brrring.* Someone had left their phone at work.

He left his seat and hunted the phone down. Like a game of hot and cold, the phone stopped just as he neared. In a drawer, it was. The top one of three built into the desk of Ursula Rawson-Sage. And locked.

He went back to his own desk and stared at the screen.

"I do wonder if anyone is thinking about you whilst you do all this thinking about us," Constance had said to him. "Though I do promise you, Mr Povey, nobody *is* thinking about you. They're only thinking about themselves."

The phone started up again. This time, Jake went to the drawer armed with a knife.

*

Jake had only been here once. A barbeque, three, maybe four summers back, when Ursula was still married to her husband and had just hit fifty. He had not taken Della, couldn't remember if he'd even told Della where he was going, but he was over an hour late and there was a choice of skinny-pink sausages or charred chicken thighs served up on sheets of kitchen roll that'd stuck to the skin. It was brand new and desirable, the schools were outstanding, and two of the four bedrooms were en-suite. The garage could take three cars at a push, her eldest was a year off driving lessons, so it was, until then, the pool room, where her sons were sent to chill out. At least that's what Ursula had been saying as Jake had shyly approached to say, "Well, hello there," and little else.

This time there would be no pleasantries. No tour of the house. No admiring of the back lawn. Jake kept his finger on the bell until the door was opened by a woman (not Ursula) shouting - *Alright, alright! I'm coming!* - and she greeted him with a spatula and a butcher's apron. Jake pushed her aside and walked straight in calling out Ursula's name.

She was in the kitchen. A glass of red. A cigarette. Still in her work clothes. Billy Bragg CD on low. She turned and saw Jake, "Povey!" but nothing else as he was already waving the mobile phone at her, Ursula's wife now coming to grab Jake by the arm and shouting that she would called the police.

"Call them," Jake said, the phone still held aloft. "I've got plenty to tell them. Haven't I, Ursula?"

Ursula looked at the phone in Jake's hand. Then she turned away, picked up her cigarette and dragged on it hard. "It's ok, love. He's from work," gesturing for them to be left alone. There was some reluctance, quickly abated, the police apparently not going to be called unless needed, and the kitchen door was shut with the words, "I'm only in here if you want me."

Ursula smiled at the door then turned about. "She's terribly protective. More than any man I've ever known." She smiled. "Can I get you a drink?"

"How long?" Jake had not come here to drink.

Ursula sucked in her breath. "Couple of years. Maybe three." She finished the wine in her glass and poured a lot more back in. "It's not what you think."

"No. It's probably worse."

She smiled into her wineglass and began:

"His father disowned him, you know. He was perhaps eleven, twelve years old. He went to live at Bennett Road. Slept on a camp-bed in the front room because of something that'd happened to a friend of theirs; he'd drowned I think. But it wasn't because of the drowned boy that he'd been disowned. It was because he'd robbed from a sweet-shop which had somehow led to the drowned boy. And all he'd robbed was just over four pounds - £12.50 in today's money - but that was that. He was beaten to a pulp by his dad and Constance took him in and brought him back to life. He lived there for almost five years. Like family, he says, and Constance always said that he was just coming home."

She paused to drink from her wine. "Still, she kept him out of the care system and he won't ever see them on the streets, but he's like a cat with a mouse when it comes to Totty." She turned to look at Jake. "You know, not all animals lay down their lives for their young like we do," switching to supervision patter. "Some animals only ever bear two offspring just to ensure one lives." She drank more wine. "Some say that Joss is his. Some say so is Kirty. But they're not. Malcolm Gandy knows where to draw the line and he'll take a brick over a woman any day."

"What the fuck has this got to do with anything?" seethed Jake.

"Because whatever you think Povey, I'm always on the side of the children. Not the state. Not the system. The children. And I don't much care what side Malcolm Gandy sits on as long as every door is on the latch and there's spare keys under the mat. Because a pissed off Gandy will get over being used. A colleague feeling let down will move on. But a neglected or, God forbid, abused and nearly-dead child will not."

"You're cooking the books with Malcolm fucking Gandy! You're selling confidential information to him."

"Yes I am," she said flatly. "But I have kids too Povey. And I just want what's best."

Jake stepped towards her and pushed the phone in her face. "You're a liar," he spat.

"He gives me access to houses. I slip him the nod when I know what's coming up and empty. I'm then able to re-house certain clients who need long-term refuge or a short-term facade for the purpose of court hearings. I gave one to Totty Minton, for instance, and he lived there on the paper until the judge ordered him sole custody of his kids. Then he went home." She shrugged and carried on.

"Gandy doesn't give a fuck who's in them. People come. People go. He gets his rent. I get a safeguarding godsend when housing fobs me off because apparently the situation isn't life threatening enough. There used to be enough houses to go round. Then there wasn't. So I picked up the phone to a man who had houses on tap because I was getting really scared of what we couldn't provide." She drained her glass. "And we could get in there quickly. Some women liked knowing that. Felt safer than they'd ever done in their lives."

She made her way to a French dresser where wineglasses filled a shelf. She grabbed the stem of one and filled it with red wine. She handed it to Jake and then replenished her own. She chinked his glass and smiled. "If you can't beat 'em, join 'em," sipping at her wine. "But you do whatever you have to do."

She put on oven gloves and bent down to open the oven door. She pulled out a chicken, roasting with lemon, garlic, and thyme. "You're welcome to stay and eat with us," she said, patting the chicken with her fingers, shaking the tray, returning it to the shelf and closing the door. "Though I'm sure a handsome boy like you has got someone to go home to. Maybe a pregnant girl?" She removed the oven gloves and held out her hand. "It would be easier for you to give me the phone back but..." she paused and shrugged again. "I'll understand if you want to keep it."

Jake looked down at the phone. The glass of wine. He looked up at Ursula.

"You know, some people stay in the system because it's all they know and some people really do need us," she bit her lip. "I do it all for the right reasons Povey. I can promise you that."

"And Bennett Road?"

"Ah, now that *was* a favour. Call it legal paperwork."

"You used me."

"We're all *used* Povey."

"It's not right!"

"No. Two kids sleeping on camp-beds in the middle of a front room in 21st century Britain isn't right. As it won't be right that when Constance goes, Joss will be bringing up Kirty because Totty can't do it and Lux will be on the next plane out. Besides, the way he's going he's either heading for the woods to copy his father or we'll be organising play dates in the nick."

"So where are they going?"

"What does it matter?"

"Because it's my case. Call it legal paperwork."

Ursula hooted with laughter. "Oh Povey," she grinned. "Pulled the poor working class matriarch on you did she? Where do you think Kirty gets all her ideas from? Or did she cartwheel around your heart too?" She went to the kitchen door and opened it, leant on the doorframe and called - "Dinner!" - to the rest of the house. "Last chance to sit at my table," she said, turning back to Jake. "Or you're on your own."

Jake started laughing. He shook his head then bent down to the oven, opened its door and chucked the mobile phone inside. Said, "I resign," and made his way out into the night.

Saturday 8th May

2010

Round 28

Constance switched on the wireless to check the time. *You're listening to Signal. Here is the news*: The one with the least votes has become the kingmaker. Nick Clegg could finally spin – "I'm with the band."

She looked up at the kitchen clock: twenty past four. Her alarm clock had told her earlier that it was ten past seven. She went back over to the radio and turned it up. That'd been the eight o'clock news. It seemed that no-one could make a decision on the time either, and she set about filling the kettle knowing that later on Totty would replace the batteries in the kitchen clock for her. Then it suddenly occurred to her that he wouldn't. He might not be back in time.

She padded over to the pantry for the step-ladder. It was a noisy, clattering contraption at the best of times, but this morning it sounded particularly grating: because who declares when a bed is a bed, when a house makes a home, how a family should live? And she outstretched the ladder legs underneath the wall clock and set about climbing its four rungs.

Halfway up and she felt giddy; her balance completely awry. She put her best foot forward, tried to lift it up a rung towards the ladder's small platform where she might feel safer. But her foot wouldn't move. She couldn't feel her foot. And, if she wasn't mistaken, her kettle wasn't boiling either.

Round 29

Granddad's glasses, clipboard, lipstick, and what looked like a pair of her mother's left-behind heels on her feet: Kirty Minton, stood upon what she called her tooth-brushing stool, looked into the bathroom mirror and said, "Good morning ladies and gentlemen," holding out her small hand. "Welcome to Minton Houses, for sale and to let. On my checking list today is furniture, keys, lights, hot water, and dog hairs. I'm a scrupulous checker because the last house we lived in had no oven door and the radiators cried in the night. And then in the one before that, the lady had forgotten her cats and to leave us the curtains. But today, we're on the change," and she pulled out a set of keys from her pyjama pocket, its little plastic nametag fluttering between her fingers. "So ladies and gentlemen," she declared, jangling the keys at her reflection in the mirror. "I give you the future. I give you Fairview."

Gold and shiny and just freshly-cut, Kirty pressed one of the keys down on the palm of her hand then traced the indent with her finger. She did the same with the other key on her other hand and then, holding up both palms in front of her, studied both key-marks in the mirror.

"The thing about keys," she said. "Is that big keys don't mean big houses," and she waved her hands in front of her, two little pink keys on her palms side by side. "What's that you say madam?" she asked herself, nodding furiously. "Oh I agree. If wishes were houses I'd have three too; one for the chickens and one that's for Nan, and a third one that Mr Gandy doesn't know about," and she put her fingers to her lips and said, "*Shhh.*"

"Oh indeed," she carried on at herself. "I don't know why we've got to move again either," and she adjusted her glasses and looked down at her clipboard. "But of course," she said. "We're as common as muck."

Kirty jumped off her tooth-brushing stool and knelt down on the bathroom floor aside of the white plastic bath panel. She nudged the left hand bottom corner with the palm of her hand and watched as it flipped towards her, making her able to push her small hand underneath and reach inside.

She pulled out an old toilet bag. Small, pink floral and drawstring, it had been her mother's, left behind in the rush and found by Kirty on the bathroom floor. Now, it was Kirty's toilet bag and she used it to store all the things she didn't want anyone else to know about. She pulled them out one by one ticking the boxes in her mind:

A lipstick-stained fag-butt she sometimes pretended to smoke.

A sequinned butterfly grip she sometimes pushed into her hair.

A piece of broken plate (Minton, April design) - smashed by her daddy for a pact - *a piece for you, a piece for Joss, a piece for me - see? We come together. We're all in this together.*

A miniature bottle of Smirnoff vodka (empty); what her mother used to keep in her handbag telling Kirty that she was like Alice in Wonderland and going to grow so big one day that the world would have to look up to her.

A thinning silver bangle - not even real silver, it used to leave green stains about Lux's right wrist.

A Polaroid, the picture pinking and yellowing from the damp. Not of her mother but of her, just three days old and in Joss' arms as he cradled her for the first time on the settee.

Oh, and her birth certificate. The only thing in the world that called her by her real name.

She sat back on her haunches and mulled the keys over in her hands. They were such a set of troublemakers. Every time a new set of keys arrived she was made to pack up her rucksack and wear her home on her back like a snail when she was already at home. Her little mind couldn't take anymore houses.

She was just about to add the keys to her bag of trinkets when she heard a sort of crash-bang coming up from under the floorboards, as if something metal had clattered onto the kitchen floor. And was that her grandmother calling out?

She pushed the bath panel back into place and jumped up to flush the toilet. She put the keys back in her pocket and went to open the door. But the noises had finished. The house was quiet other than a pair of arguing voices on the kitchen radio. She stood back on her tooth-brushing stool, looked up at her reflection and wiped her brow.

"Phew," she said. "That was close," and then allowed her face to break into a beaming smile. "Of course I'll show you round," she said. "Would you like me to start upstairs or down?"

Round 30

It was a most compromising position to find yourself in. One leg trapped between the rungs of a step ladder, the other somewhere underneath your buttocks, bent but not broken, painful but not unbearable; Constance had been trying to reach for the light switch to check if the electric was off or if there'd been a power cut in the night, and she'd had her fingers at full stretch. But then she'd lost her balance and then her footing, and one leg had given way at the knee whilst the other had slipped through the first and second rungs as she fell. The only way out of this embarrassing predicament was to lift the step ladder away from her body. That not only meant that someone would find her looking like this, but that she'd also nothing to hold onto with her right hand. And she had to hold onto something because she couldn't feel her right arm, and holding onto the cold metal with her left hand meant that she could keep telling herself she was still alive. She could feel something. I can feel something cold. And then she'd got so very cross with herself, because what she should've done was come down from the step ladder one step at a time, left the kitchen clock for Totty to sort out and simply tried the light switch instead of trying to kill two birds with one step ladder. Now, she was afraid that if she let go of the step ladder, for the urge to use her left hand to rub some life back into her right was overwhelming, the step ladder would topple onto her shoulders, pin her down to the kitchen floor and give her grandchildren their first indication that she was not very well. But now there were pins and needles to deal with in her right foot, and excruciating pins and needles at that, so there was nothing else for it but to try and kick-away the step ladder. Which she did, on the count of three, and that was the clattering noise that Kirty had heard reverberating through the bathroom floorboards, but had chosen to do nothing about it because she was very busy being someone else on her tooth-brushing stool. However, Constance was not exactly free of the step ladder. She had only managed to shift its position so that it now lay across her left shin, which she couldn't feel, and her left thigh, which she could most certainly feel, because goodness that step ladder was heavy!

And it wasn't right that she wasn't given another voting slip when she'd made a mistake and not voted for the left. She was also, somehow, still clinging onto the bottom rung with her left hand telling herself cold, I feel cold, this ladder is cold, and the only thing left to do was sit it out. Or she could reach out for that tea-towel over there and pretend she was down there cleaning the kitchen floor and the step ladder was both useful and intentional to the task, which meant a whole lot of refocusing her mind in order to get her working hand to let go of the ladder and reach for the tea-towel, which she might just be able to reach at full stretch. It would hurt, by God it would hurt, and she must prepare herself for that, but she would do so by focusing on the radio where the re-elected Councillor Roy Dingwall was telling her that it was only a crisis if you make it into a crisis; that it was, in his mind, a conservative government that must be allowed to get on with running the country, and that affordable housing was to be a parliamentary priority. And no, he told the radio presenter trying to get him to bite. There has been nothing un-parliamentary about the social housing situation around here.

Round 31
Eggs

There
must be an aisle for eggs.
Don't eat that egg it's your father's!
Don't egg the pudding. Don't over-egg the flan.
Constance was full of old wives' tales told egg-shaped.
The last egg left from the Saturday bake: Madeira cake.
Always plain old Madeira cake, Slather with best butter. Cup of
tea. *You'll take a cup of tea, won't you? Slice of cake?* Dull, stoic
Ned, home from a Saturday morning's bulltime. He'd spend over half
an hour in the bathroom. His hands in the potty soaking them in his own
urine to harden up the skin. Back downstairs, easy clothes now, braces
about his hips, old fashioned, *The old fashioned ways are the best.* Now
scrubbing at his hands, sniffing his fingers, more soap, sniffing again. "Son
pass me the towel" – making a meal out of drying his hands. My towel. His
eggs. No-one's father. Ned had no way to fertilise an egg. He knew it and
Constance knew it, and Ned knew that Totty knew, but Constance didn't know
that Ned had told him. *Son, you're not mine.* Totty left wondering – did he buy
that rope because of shame? Or because Constance thought she'd convinced Ned
Totty was his despite knowing he probably couldn't? Even so, Ned had died a
working class snob when it came to reproduction, unable to forgive his wife for
wanting another man's runt of a son, more than she ever needed him. Totty stared
at the eggs. Twelve types. Green boxes, yellow boxes, blue boxes, grey. He
could count them not read them, knew what was small, medium, and large. He
picked up a long grey box. Factory hens. Cheap as chips. Egg and chips. A
dozen little eggs all in a row. Totty opened up his toolbox and began to
fill it with eggs from grey boxes. As many as he could. And since
no-one asked him what the hell he was doing, He filled it up
to the top, glad he'd opted for the Express store
opposite the radio station, Because damn!
Those eggs were heavy.

Councillor lashes out at Lone Activist

Protester says "Egging Roy Dingwall is a criminal offence but egging me is a policy" before battering disgraced councillor with eggs

Newly-elected Conservative Councillor Roy Dingwall was said to be "rattled but doing ok" after being pelted with a blatter of eggs by a lone protester as he left a local radio station earlier this afternoon.

The station's security guard John Craig (53) said he watched in horror as Mr Dingwall, having been hit in the face "several times" by a barrage of eggs, was then seen to scuffle with the protester who was, according to Mr Craig, manacled to a galvanised metallic toolbox. A 44 year-old unnamed man was taken into local police custody but no formal charges have been made.

In an exclusive interview with *The Sentinel,* Craig, visibly shaken by the experience, spoke of how the protester came out of nowhere and "lobbed egg after egg" whilst chanting "go to work on an egg ha ha, go to work on an egg hee hee", until Mr Dingwall grabbed him by the scruff of the neck and punched him in the shoulder. The man, according to Craig, "went down like a ton of bricks and looked winded." Mr Dingwall's spokespeople told *The Sentinel* that Mr Dingwall was acting in pure self-defence and defied anyone to *not* do the same in similar circumstances.

Mr Dingwall later confirmed to *The Sentinel* that he had been attacked by what he termed "a lone activist with a toolbox full of eggs," and understood that he was being detained for questioning. He declined to comment any further on the matter but thanked his constituency for all their good wishes saying, "I've listened. I've learnt. I'm humbled. I will do my best for the most," and that he welcomed public input via his website www.roydingwall.net. "It is," he said, "your homeland, your Stoke, your society. It is only a broken one when you break rank."

Round 32

Charcoal suit. Purple tie. Matt black brogues fresh out of the box: Frank's three-bed semi-detached was so far up Gandy's street it warranted new shoes, and he stepped inside with the glee of a man who was about to begin an affair after a long time thinking about it.

"Frank."

"Malcolm."

It was a jumpy handshake.

"This is a turn up."

"Only speculative."

"On the cards though."

"Only in your mind, Malcolm, most of us buy houses to live in them."

"And it goes in one ear, comrade, out the other, and straight into the bank."

Entrance Hallway: UPVC double glazed door with sad panel effect. Under stairs linen cupboard. Staircase with balustrades and spindles. Radiator. Telephone point. Part-carpeted stairs.

Frank and Gandy tolerated one another, neither love nor hatred lost. Gandy saw Frank as a clearance sale sort of chap, a life lived in 4th place. Frank thought Gandy an urban infection worming his way up from the manholes. Gandy followed Frank upstairs with the word "potential" on the tip of his tongue, the phrase "reserve all judgements" in the back of his mind, and wondered for the wallpaper. He'd seen it somewhere before and hadn't admired it then either.

Bedroom One: *12'6" x 10'10"* Built in double wardrobe with dressing mirror and drawer accommodation below. Sissy's clothes still hanging in one wardrobe. Make-up bag and hair tongs on dressing table how she'd left them. Telephone point. Radiator. UPVC double glazed window looking to front of property.

"I tried to resign yesterday," said Frank, as he pushed open the bedroom door. "You know what my gaffer said to me? He said, "solid copper like you Frank, with your knowledge of the spivs, tits, and traffic cones round here? I don't think so,"" and he waved a long white envelope at Gandy. "Gave it me back, said, "You're embarrassing me and you're embarrassing yourself." I'd been up all bloody night writing the damn thing, wording it right, and then it's thrown back in my bloody face," and he shook his head, the two of them now stood either side of the bed – Frank on the left still mourning, Gandy on the right thinking cold and starkly furnished and reeking of a man coming home with sick on his shoes.

"So I asks him to sack me on the grounds of gross misconduct," Frank presses on. "I said, "I haven't done a day's honest graft for the force since I lost my wife. I pay young Charlene to fiddle my paperwork. I've got a dirty fucking nose when it comes to Bennett Road, and I've just kept a dickhead mate out of the clink again because they'd have his fucking kids off him otherwise." You know what he says to me? "That's the thing about you Frankie. You know who you are and you're reliable enough to never want any more than that." So I tell him that I'm out hunting every night with nearly two hundred grand's worth of surveillance equipment and I'm armed. "By God I'm armed," I tell him. "I'm hunting them all down. Every drunk-driver I can find.""

He turned away from the window and found Gandy looking at a photograph: the one with the beer stain clouding the bride's face. The one where Sissy had thought herself too old and too knowing for white and had opted for a mauve cashmere two-piece from Dorothy Perkins' petite section, more Blackpool ballroom than bride. She'd done her own hair with hot tongs and there was no matron of honour, no father to give her away. She'd carried a posy of daffs tied up with a string of ivy she'd pulled away from the back wall around the drainpipe and her shoes were something blue that'd aggravated her bunion all day.

Gandy returned the photograph to the top of the drawers. He knew those drawers. They'd always been a restless piece of furniture, Constance shifting them from one room to the next.

"You stay in that car for one fucking reason, comrade, and that's to spite our boy Minton," his eyes still fixed on Sissy's clouded face. He'd liked Sissy. Not anything to look at but she was solid. Lippy, but solid all the same. "You've always known who mowed her down. You just can't bring yourself to do what you really need to do."

Frank hung his head. He did know. Of course he knew. He'd known three hours after it'd happened. Mostly he pretended he didn't and looked some more, as if continuing to look was keeping Sissy alive, though one thing was clear from the footage from the CCTV above the chip shop: the driver was drunk and, since she'd been drinking ever since, she probably hadn't a single memory of it even happening.

What wasn't so clear, and what had caused the print on the rewind button to be rubbed off completely, was whether Sissy had stepped in front of the car knowing just how hard it'd be to avoid her. He'd been in traffic long enough to know that not all road-kill is accidental.

Bedroom Two: *11'8" x 9'2"* Laminate flooring (unfinished). Dado rail. Radiator. UPVC double glazed window to the back with views of the extensive garden. Unused for five years.

Frank's back bedroom had nothing to say for itself. Plans had never seen the light of day, furniture was never bought, colours never chosen, and the door was quickly shut.

Bedroom Three: *6'3" x 5'8"* Dado rail. Radiator. UPVC double glazed window to the front.

It could've been an office. A study. It was meant to be the nursery. Until Sissy found out she'd left it too late.

Close the door Frank. I've never liked that room.

And then later: "We don't need a three-bed house, Frank. What's the point of having a house when you've no family to put in it? This whole place should be condemned and you should take me to Spain."

"That I will, Sissy duck. Me and you will go live the life of Riley on the Med."

Bathroom: *7'7" x 5'11"* Panelled corner bath. Low level W.C. Pedestal wash hand basin. Separate shower cubicle, separate colour to suite. Dado rail. Radiator. UPVC double glazed frosted window to the rear. All Sissy's toiletries where she left them.

"This is all a bit dramatic, though, even by your standards," and Gandy winced at the dusky pink bathroom suite, its post-war tile job, the lack of a housewife's touch and Toilet Duck. "I mean, what's it all about, eh? You have the house and boy Minton's got the family, is that it?"

"And who's to say that I haven't got Graeme Woodward coming round for a nose after you? Fletchers, Harrison, and McCartney?"

"Because none of them deal in cash and this is about Connie and Totty and you getting your hands on some quick cash. Why else would you call me in?"

But Frank was already on his way down the stairs.

Lounge: *16'8" (into recess) x 10'8" (maximum)* Brick surround and stone hearth with coal-effect gas fire. Dado rail. Two wall light points. Coving to ceiling. TV aerial and satellite point. Dark. Miserable. Plagued with damp. A room that's crying out to be lived in.

Years ago and there'd been a family living next door to the Blatchs who'd kept a kitten with a tortoiseshell coat and a hard stare. It was loved and it was fed and it slept on the little boy's head. Then when the kitten became a cat, the family upped sticks and moved away leaving the cat behind. To Frank this was a case of cruel abandonment. They should never have bought the cat in the first place. To Gandy it was a matter of options: the cat could suck up to a new family and work its way into their hearts and cat-flap, give up, or go feral. "We always get a choice comrade," Gandy had said.

Years ago, Frank Blatch and Malcolm Gandy were like two feral cats free to a good home. And years ago, Frank Blatch and Malcolm Gandy both courted the same good home until both got their feet under the kitchen table. However, though Constance Minton had use for them both, there wasn't actually room for them both, and gradually the family split three ways.

One went to the bank and hit the housing market. Another stayed at home with his mother. The third joined the police, earned a wage, bought a house, sold it, made a packet in the boom, bought another, cash, then met a girl who came with a cat and after they were married and after she'd died, the cat walked out of the house and kept going.

It was, as most things were in Frank's head, another story put there by Constance when, at his most scared, he believed all that she told him as being true in the world. Because that's what you did when you loved someone. You believed them. "God gave me two sons Frank," Constance used to say. "One to make up the deficit of the other who lets me down."

But Frank wasn't daft. Like Sissy used to say, what was the point of having a three-bed house when you'd no family to put in it? But to give it to Totty? To hand it to him on a plate?

It was gratefulness that Frank always felt for the Mintons. Gratitude, so extreme, it used to make him feel ill. Sometimes, he'd drive himself nuts with the sheer shame of never quite being able to pay back what they'd given him. And then he'd wonder: what *had* they given him?

Inclusion, Sissy called it, which could, to the lonely, be mistaken for love which, in turn, could be, and more than probably was, used in many ways to make him feel as guilty as fuck. Which he did and often. He was made to feel guilty. Guilt so powerful, it stuck to his skin. "But it isn't guilt, Frank," Sissy always assured. "It's emotional bloody blackmail, because gratitude for inclusion creates guilt then regret which eats you alive."

"One twenty then, cash," and Gandy's opening offer lacked lustre and eye contact.

"House across the road went for one sixty last month," Frank told him. "Loft's converted of course, so you'll give me one five five."

"When one two five's all it's actually worth?"

"It's worth one five eight according to Woodward."

"But we're talking cash comrade, and you're pushing your luck at one thirty."

"Fletcher's reckon I should start at one five nine."

"One three two Frankie, and that's not insulting."

"You're insulting my mother's memory comrade. The way you blew her house down, we're surely talking one five seven at the very least."

"One three five and you'll have the cash this afternoon."

Frank smiled. "All these fucking houses and yet where do you live, comrade? Where do you actually call home?"

"You're one to talk when the only thing that's missing in here is a couple of camp-beds," and Gandy headed out of the room.

Kitchen: *10' 9" x 8'8"* Fitted units with matching wall, drawer and base units. Working surfaces. 1 bowl inset sink with mixer tap. Gas cooker. Washing machine point with plumbing. Gas central heating combination boiler behind cupboard. Housing for microwave. UPVC double glazed patio door to garden. Bare cupboards. Fridge freezer thrown in as it hides a patch of wall a different colour to the rest.

Frank lit a cigarette, chucked Gandy the packet who chucked it him back. Gandy's got standards and he takes out his own cigarettes but uses Frank's lighter so as not to offend. He hands the lighter back to Frank and looks him over: his skin has rusted like a cheap metal, his stomach has bulged, his heart hasn't healed. "You'd be better off doing it up and renting it out," Gandy told Frank from the other side of the kitchen. "It'll make you money without moving an inch because it's a decent family home is this. You've just no idea how to live in it."

"Then a family should have it,"

"But not just any family, eh?"

"I'm under no obligation, comrade."

"And neither am I."

"That family has had enough out of me."

"So selling your house to me is you walking away?"

"When you want Jerusalem."

"I'm not here to buy your guilt, Frank."

"But you'll buy my services alright."

"I only ever buy what's on offer."

Frank stubbed out his cigarette on a saucer. "Then you'll need a new friend," he said. "And for me to keep my trap shut, I want one five five cash."

"You should be biting my hand off at one forty."

"And you should be grateful for all you receive."

"Don't be putting your pious shit on me Frankie boy."

"I've been a buffer between you and the law for over twenty years."

"And I've been grateful comrade," Gandy reminded him, rubbing his thumb against his forefingers. "*You've* been grateful."

"I've been a fucking embarrassment to my kind. I should've had you put away when I had the chance."

Frank lifted his head and looked over at Gandy just as Gandy turned to look over at Frank.

"Ok then comrade," and Gandy held out his hand. "In honour of all memories, one fifty it is. But officially they're squatting and that's against the law."

"And officially it's not my department and nor do I care. One. Five. Five."

Gandy gave this some serious thought. "One five five," he said. "And one more little bird to do some talking."

"The birds have flown, comrade. The nest is empty."

"But you're my friend Frank."

"We've never been friends."

"Then what have we been, played? Because don't think that she's not had a hand in this, Frank, because she has. Everything we do is because of Connie. She's even staged this."

"You think I care anymore?"

"I think you want two little trust funds side by side," and Gandy's scowl slackened into a useful smile. "They're someone else's kids Frank. You're trying to buy lives for someone else's kids."

"Two kids who've had fuck all as kids. At least this'll give them a start as adults."

"You're talking some serious fucking money they've no concept of."

"And why do we have his back?" Frank asked. "Why do we still do it? Guilt's a killer comrade. We're fucking riddled with it. Working class boys like us, we should know our place and that's as four little boys who pushed and shoved and ran too far from where she wanted us all to stay. You might've pushed him, but we've all got Jonty's blood on our hands. Even Connie," and he ambled past Gandy meaning to go back in the lounge, but he decided better of it.

Instead, he jotted down some numbers on a post-it for three bank accounts, also indicating how much was to be deposited in where. He handed the post-it to Gandy along with his house-keys, both sets and Sissy's, said, "Don't let me down, comrade," then he opened his front door, looked at the end of his road as if it were the first time he'd ever seen it, and headed towards it. Sold out.

Round 33

Jake Povey had rented a white van with a stiff gear stick and had been shown by a man eating meat-paste sandwiches how to release the handbrake with two hands. In the back of the van were two single beds, a circular pine table with four matching chairs, and a mustard velour settee with unappealing threads of emergency red knitted through it. It was the best of a bad bunch, a snip at the price, but it would have to do because it was the sort of place that didn't do refunds.

He'd thought of other items too. A kettle and a microwave - housewarming gifts never used - a small fridge, also a gift, a blender and a wok, two matching bedside table lamps, his kitchen wall clock, and a small chest of drawers stencilled with strawberries he used to keep in the en-suite for guests. The clothes he'd had second thoughts about. The gadgets would've given him away. He'd started up the van, went so far, then worried for how light the load felt. He told himself - it's hardly worth renting the bloody thing otherwise. He put the van in reverse and drove back home.

He came back down the stairs of his flat with two more cardboard boxes and three bin-bags full of bed linen and a king size duvet (duck-down). He'd just say that everything came as a job-lot, no questions asked, theirs to do with as they wished. As he pulled away in the van a second time, he'd thought about how a teenager might feel about wearing second-hand trainers, what kitchen utensils were relevant, whether rugs and throws were their thing. He reminded himself that he had no need for them and then realised that they might not need them either. He stopped the van and pulled over. But then everyone needs bedding. It's what they'd all said: when you've split up, you get yourself some new bedding, because no matter how many times you wash it, it will always smell of the other and linger in your sheets.

He started up the van again and continued to drive.

Round 34

"It was just a giddy spell," Constance insisted, no longer trapped by the step ladder and with the air of a dead pigeon scooped to the side of the road with a piece of cardboard. "I don't know what you're doing here Mr Povey, but please, don't make a fuss."

Kirty was to her left, a white pillowcase safety-pinned to her v-neck with its hastily drawn red felt-tip cross and an upside down defunct wristwatch of her granddad's tied on with an elastic band. She shone the headlamp into Constance's left ear and let out a deep sigh. "Beeswax," she told her grandmother. "Doctor, we're going to need cotton buds, maximum strength."

Constance told her granddaughter to run upstairs, bathroom cabinet, bottom shelf, and don't break anything. Joss handed Constance a nip of whisky and dropped into the armchair opposite. "I still think we should call an ambulance," he said. "I don't know what you thought you were doing up there. Why didn't you call me? I was only in the other room."

"And I've asked you twice now to give the electricity board a bell to see how long our electric's going to be off," Constance snapped, taking a sip of the whisky. "Yet you still haven't managed to do that."

Joss turned to Jake. "You could take her to the hospital, couldn't you? You said you had a van."

Constance waved away the suggestion quickly. "I'm eighty-five," she said. "I'm always doing things I don't know that I'm doing," but then she had to turn away because this was a part where she could no longer act anymore.

It had been embarrassing. Of all people. Constance had no idea for how long she'd been under that step ladder or for why Jake Povey

was suddenly in front of her offering both his hands and saying –
"Careful now, that's it, steady as, one foot in front of the other." At
first, she wasn't entirely sure it was him – him out of work clothes,
her out of sorts – she could've been imagining the whole thing. But it
was him and she'd cried out, not in alarm but in severe pain; her right
foot not exactly coming to life, and that blasted kitchen clock, the
cause of it all, telling her that life had stopped anyway at twenty past
four.

"Really," a poky little voice hiding all-sorts. "Please don't fuss, *I'm
fine.*"

She had instantly tried to make tea. "You'll take some tea today
won't you Mr Povey?" forgetting the lack of electricity. But her right
knee had given way again and she'd dropped to the floor. She'd cried
out a second time, more pain, a different pain, a cruel pain, and as
she'd gone down, knock-kneed, jelly-legged, Jake had caught her by
the arms and thrown her left arm about his shoulders – "Hold on now
Mrs Minton, all in good time" - and what could she do but hold on?

But not for long. Here was Joss, striding into the kitchen, pulling
out his headphones, calling out to Jake – "What are *you* doing here?"
– And then – "Nan! Are you ok? Oh my God, what's happened?
What's happened? Is she dying?" - the panic in his voice attracting Kirty
who descended the stairs two at a time, clearing the last three,
running into the kitchen then running back upstairs to amend her
outfit. She was back in the kitchen as a makeshift nurse, a roll of
Elastoplast tucked under her right arm.

"No, I'm not dying," stubborn as you like. "I just got a bit stuck
that's all. Now stop fussing and please, one of you, make some tea
for Mr Povey before he thinks I've brought you both up with no
manners."

But there was no need for tea. No electricity either. "I'm not here
as a social worker, Mrs Minton," Jake attempted to explain. "I'm here
as a friend."

Constance sniffed. "You're not our friend Mr Povey, but we are on
your conscience. I don't doubt that for a minute," and she gestured
for her grandchildren to leave them alone in the kitchen.

Pots piled up in the sink; a frying pan of bacon fat left to sulk on the stove; a single egg on a piece of kitchen roll looking as if it might roll and smash; it had the air of a truck stop, people passing through, some not coming home at all. "Are you here to catch us out?" Constance asked him quietly.

"I'm here to help," Jake replied, and started to roll up his sleeves.

Because he was. He really was. He'd realised that on Thursday night when sat in accident and emergency. An accidental pregnancy. An emergency caused by the son she adored despite all he did and didn't do: Jake had realised so much that night and vowed to change it all. He'd driven Della home to her mother's in silence. They'd sat in the car outside the house and locked hands over the gearstick. Not for long. A minute or two at most. But it was enough for them both to realise that whatever they had had between them had gone. Della had let him go first.

She'd said, "I can do this on my own Jake. Actually, I'd prefer it if I could." She'd smiled. "Call it aspiration."

He'd said, "Forget about the mortgage. What I said."

She'd said, "I already have."

She'd got out of the car and he'd watched her walk slowly into her mother's house without turning around once and, as he had, he'd gone back. Twenty-three years in fact, to when he was told *it's a girl*. His mother sorting out the legal paperwork in the hospital waiting room with a sour look, his father shaking the hand of the other father - "You don't expect to be grandparents at thirty-eight." Jake choosing, there and then, not to see the child.

His daughter Abi lived up in Liverpool. She'd done university, BA, MA. Had stuck around for a young man who'd apparently, recently, let her down. She was mulling over her options in the student union. Coming home *wasn't* an option. Travelling maybe. All this education, all these qualifications, and she'd found no more than a job behind the bar in the university that was supposed to have prepared her for work. She would call soon. It's all she ever said. *I'll call soon.* Quick text messages sent on the hoof. Jake had resisted the urge to drive up to Liverpool there and then to save her and had, instead, driven back to Bennett Road and sat outside No. 13, as if staring at the drawn curtains at the front window where he knew slept a fifteen year old boy and a seven year old girl on camp-beds would tell him exactly what to do next.

He'd eventually realised that it wasn't about saving but *savings*. And so he'd driven home and transferred a lot of his own into his daughter's bank account. Then, he set up a second account for another little girl who would come into the world to find it even harder without any savings of her own. I am buying them aspiration, he told himself, not their thanks and not their love. Because in this world of ideals, if you didn't get a good start in life you didn't stand a chance in ever catching up. Then he'd typed out a formal resignation letter. Drank a little whisky, begun to pack up his flat.

"They are moving today though, right?" Jake now asked Constance. "It's just that I have some stuff, in a van, that I thought might be of use, I don't know," and he hid the rest of what he meant to say in a small cough.

Constance raised her eyebrows. "Stuff?"

"Beds, furniture, you know. Stuff he might need to kit out the new place."

"I see."

"Second-hand, but as good as new, and I had the keys to the van and I thought," he paused. "Well, I wasn't sure what he had and what he needed."

Constance smiled. "You're too young to have lived through a war," she began. "But wars do us the world of good, Mr Povey. It puts a stop to all this yours and mine and what we think we need."

"I'm not looking down on you Mrs Minton," and it'd come out too quickly. "I just want to help."

"You should write novels if you want to romanticise the poor," her tone considerably crass. "Don't you think we've jumped through enough hoops for you as it is?"

Jake offered a bleary little smile. "I am your ally here," he murmured. "I am rooting for you."

"Then what are you really doing here on a Saturday, Mr Povey? Have you not your own life to live?" Another sip of whisky. "Because how old are you, duck? Where's your wedding ring? Why aren't you taking your young lad out to the match?"

"You do know that Malcolm Gandy is stitching you up?"

"I think we're done here, aren't we Mr Povey?"

"All those referrals to us, what Lux is saying, they're all from him one way or the other. None of them are founded. I know that for sure. It's why..."

"You'll appreciate why I can't walk you to the door."

"Mrs Minton, you're not listening."

"Oh but I am Mr Povey. And I think you lot have done enough now, don't you?"

Jake closed his eyes. He wanted to admit to her - *I've resigned because of you. Don't you see how you've made me see?* But the words seemed so insulting. So he told her that it would do no harm for her to take a look. It wasn't as if it was *his stuff*. It was just some stuff that he'd come across and loaded into a van for the taking. House clearances, goodwill gestures, that sort of thing. Better for them to have something than nothing.

"And you think that's what they have Mr Povey? You think my family has nothing?"

"That's not what I said, Mrs Minton."

"Stuff isn't what we need."

"You could still take a look."

He was surprised that she'd followed him out. She'd even held onto his shirtsleeve with her fingertips. It was as much of a crutch as she could bear to allow. He unlocked the van doors and flung them wide.

"That's a lot of stuff Mr Povey," said Constance, as she steadied herself against the van door and peered in. "I can see it's been weighing you down."

Jake looked down at the pavement. "Like you say Mrs Minton, what you don't need."

"He does try, you know," Constance interrupted, as she lifted up a dust sheet to reveal a nest of tables. "But even with all this lovely stuff dotted about the place, he won't be able to keep it." She let the dust sheet fall. "I am proud of him Mr Povey, I have to be. But some people are just meant for the bottom of the heap. You do understand that, don't you?" And she stepped away from the van so that Jake could close its doors.

It was the shutting of the right van door that revealed Totty. He looked so much smaller than normal. Worn down. Weary. Harrowed. His overalls were splattered in blood, sweat, paint, and cracked eggs. His left arm sagged from the weight of the toolbox, the weight of his world, and he stared straight through Jake as if he couldn't see him at all.

"Son," said Constance. "I didn't see you there."

"Well, I'm small enough to fit into your pocket, aren't I?" and Totty lifted up his toolbox with both hands and started to run.

*

He wasn't meant to be that small, but then there was no such thing as sperm banks back then. Choice didn't come into it. And though it wasn't premeditated, for Ben Gandy could crack a mirror, he'd had his eye on Constance since he was sixteen years old.

She had wept afterwards, for some time as it happens, her hands covering her face and her legs pulled up towards her chest. She hadn't undressed fully, though he had and quickly. In fact, she was not only wearing a polo neck, but her factory tabard, her girdle, and greyest bra. There was no love felt on her part as she'd lifted up her skirt. Rather, it'd been a means to an end on the spur of the moment, and whilst he went hell for leather atop of her - for dreams really did come true - Constance had recited all the cleaning products on the shelves in Shoestringer's Grocers in her head, and even put them into alphabetical order.

Before he came, he asked her to say something dirty. "Whisper it Connie," he'd said. "Whisper it like you mean it."

And so she'd pulled his left earlobe close and asked, "How long is this going to take? I've a pile of ironing to get through."

He still brought her flowers the next day. A little plastic posy tied up with brown string and a packet of sugared almonds to take the taste away. He left them on the back doorstep whilst she hid from him in the pantry, and later on, she knelt in front of her mother's grave, stuck the posy in the ground, and ate those sugared almonds one by one by one until she was sick on the dandelions. It was a good sign by all accounts.

She'd told Ned two months later, "I think we might be pregnant duck." He'd looked straight at her belly and said, "Right."

Though good old dead Ned, used to living on peanuts, could only ever write down the words some eighteen years later, finally coming clean that, "We, Connie, didn't produce anything of worth."

But to her mind they had. Totty was hers. And only hers. And it was time he knew. Heard it all from her. How she'd sort of loved Ned as he'd sort of loved her, but how she'd ached for a child as the cancer ached in her breast. How she'd thought about who to go to - who would help, who'd be right - how she'd written out list after list of pros and cons and considered all options, but what did it matter who she went to? God gave her a son. *My son.* So little and weak with a withered left hand: what did it all matter when he was her son?

My son.

She had recruited. Constance will admit that. Frank. Malcolm. Jonty.

A lion's courage. A tin heart. A little grey matter, and all just in case God took back what he should never have given.

My son. She had never allowed him to be anything else.

So Constance went after her son so much faster than she should for a woman of her age. She went with no thought for the morning's drama, for the small stroke that had attempted to claim her right side, for the cancer chomping at the bit, and though the stroke had not taken her, it had weakened her, and her right leg suddenly collapsed from under her as she got to the precinct where she slipped on a chip just outside of Keith Mo's takeaway. She went down hard and with a frightening crack.

Her first instinct was to get up. People had seen her, watched her go down. She had most certainly exposed her petticoat. But there was a searing pain travelling up her spine and nothing on the right of her would move. She put out a hand to save her. But there was no hand. Her head hit the concrete and all she could think before she passed out was that after everything she'd suffered and all she'd survived, it was a good old-fashioned chip that'd finally brought her down in the world.

Except someone was clutching her hand and telling her to hold on tight.

Saturday night,
Sunday morning

Round 35

Totty's first memory wasn't something he told a lot of people. Like all memories, what was true and what were the facts didn't always coincide, but it was dramatic enough to hold Kirty transfixed, for his mother to be rewarded time after time for her lifesaving skills, and for Totty to spend hours considering if he really had been saved.

He was around three years old, and what Totty remembers most clearly is being stood in the parlour window looking out with a pain in his left arm. The night before he'd been up at the hospital having his tonsils out, and come the morning he'd been freezing cold yet his forehead burned up like a fire poker. He'd been standing in the front window, his forehead slapped on the pane, the pain in his arm getting worse and worse, and that night, his mother and father had to save his life. They used three loaves of bread and butter as poultices, which left dark pink marks on his skin in the shape of cups and saucers, and then the next afternoon and when he woke up, the doctor told them his pneumonia had gone.

"But you mind him now," the doctor had said. "You mind everyday how he goes."

Ned had assured the doctor that his son would be minded enough, but even though the doctor had been kindly, he was told to never grace their door again.

What Totty cannot quite remember is what happened after that. Did he just get better? Did he always ail like he did because of what happened that night? And why did he only remember a lot more when standing, as he was now, at No.1 Bennett Road?

Like it wasn't just pneumonia. That his father had stopped with the poultices to tell his wife that maybe they should just let nature take its course. That the doctor who came was not that sort of doctor but a psychiatrist brought round to check for madness. That what came afterwards was the long, long silence between him and Ned as if there was simply no conversation to be had.

And yet Totty had not lived a quiet life on Bennett Road. How could you when at No.1 people came and went. *Her* on the corner, *him* on the end; it'd been a halfway place. The place after the one they'd escaped from and the one before they settled down. Totty would be warned to stay away. Folk at No. 1 were trouble and brought trouble. But Totty homed in on them, relishing the pathetic: he made those who wished to live their lives unnoticed noticed, otherwise no-one would've taken a blind bit of notice of him. The council had given the place to Gandy for a pound.

No.2 had been the Arkinstalls. He was a drunk. She'd brawl in the street. He dropped dead at fifty. Some say he came for her within the year. An Asian family moved in. Akhtar, their name was. Shake your hand every time he met you. *What's that smell?* Curry. *How do you know you don't like if you won't try it?* Akhtar was a taxi driver. Then he had a taxi firm. Taxis up and down the road blocking everyone's daylight, getting on everyone's wick. Curry and exhaust fumes. Oil spills and kids washing his cabs for driving lessons. Akhtar bought a couple of garages in the end. Then increased his fleet. Gandy wooed him with a big three-storey place on the Dividy Road. Commercial premises downstairs, living quarters upstairs, and a forecourt for the vehicles across the way. Gandy had a 30% share in Akhtar's Taxis. The forecourt, he'd said, hadn't come as cheap as he'd first thought.

No.3 had all been loud speakers. They talked all day as if each one of them were deaf, and sometimes all through the night. Worthy their name was. And they were. Worthy of a lot more than they ever had. Totty remembers: rhubarb stalks dunked in cups of sugar. Sitting on the doorstep knock-kneed whilst their mothers went the bingo. Pop and crisps every Friday night. There was only Kathleen Worthy left when Gandy knocked the door back in 2008. She held out for forty grand then went to live with one of her daughters down Telford way. Got one of them annexes apparently; bus stop right outside their house.

No.4 were the Capewells. Ian and Eleanor. Thin as rakes. Downturned mouths. She could speak French. No-one ever knew why. He'd never a done a day's work in his life. Was first in the queue when disability living allowance got introduced. Ned had no time for them. Constance even less. Gandy gave them a bungalow in the end with all these ramps, hoists, and handlebars, somewhere just off the Queensway, traffic roaring past. But they'd got a decent garden and a carer who came three times a day. They were still suing Gandy for being mis-sold. They hadn't assumed the outskirts of town meant skirting the slip-road off the M6. Gandy said the location was made more than clear in the small print. Ian Capewell tried to sue the opticians for misdiagnosis of his short-sightedness.

No.5 were called Cartwright. Washing would hang out on their line for days. Totty had been sweet on their daughter Louise. Constance would've liked him to marry Louise but she ended up 6ft 1' with spondylosis in her lower vertebrae. She owns a sandwich shop now, top of Lime Bank, 'Best Baps'. Totty used to drop in for a quick flirt and a butty, say - "If I had my time again I'd have you up that aisle in a flash" - then scoot round the corner to sign on. They did a moonlight flit last August did the Cartwrights. Better to do that than face Constance who said she felt very let down by old friends.

No.6 were Violet and Roger Baggerley. Always swanking, telling you what everything cost. Vi told everyone that her son was a businessman. He was always doing - "ever so well, Connie. You should see the size of his new company car." But Totty regularly saw him at the Jobcentre panning for gold. They put up a good fight and were going nowhere until Gandy offered to throw in a new house for their boy. They packed up and never even knocked to say ta-ra.

No.7 had been chirpy sorts. He did the night shift, she did the day. They'd pass in the street of a morning;

(Him) *Morning duck, looks like rain*

(Her) *Fetch that washing in and don't eat my eggs. I'm baking Saturday. Mother's coming.*

(Him) *Christ. What does she want now?*

Their relationship grounded in the weather and the dread of each other's mothers. Both now dead, ever so long ago. Gandy had bought their bricks for a pound.

No. 8. had been there donkeys until he went in a home, or he put her in a home. Either way, one of them lost their marbles and the house had to look after itself. Another easy target for Gandy.

No.9 had been Lesley Drive. She'd nursed through the war. Nursed through the strikes. Nursed plenty through the post-war blues and night terrors. Nursed a stray mutt with three legs she called Pogo after she'd found him under one of the wheels of Akhtar's cabs. Nursed everybody until she got sick herself. No-one nursed her. She died in her own bed though. Lot to be said for that. Constance called her a do-gooder. Salt of the earth. Had a pill for everything. "I shall miss her," Constance said. A nephew in Tasmania inherited her house. He'd never even heard of Stoke-on-Trent and when he Google-mapped it he decided he'd probably not be rushing to live there either. He was the first to sell to Gandy. Got the ball rolling, so to speak.

No.10 Keithy Harries and Marge. Brother and sister, left to fend for themselves when their mother dropped dead of a heart defect back in the day when defects weren't found and fancy illnesses had no names. Marge was a busty tub of a woman who turned their front parlour into a hairdressers. Constance went there every other Tuesday for a perm and a rinse, took Totty once every three months for a short-back and sides, and Keithy would invite him to have a look at his airgun; the last rabbit shot, skinned and hanging up by its ears in the shed. Both of them were in a home by the time Gandy looked them up. Neither of them had any idea for what they were putting their signatures to.

No.11 and Totty remembers peephole bras and fluffy slippers. Rose petal perfume and candles. Taxis parping outside - *Parp! Parp!* - some walking out with their heads held high, others on their hands and knees in the dark. But it was all very tasteful and people had to be inventive what with work being so scarce. Still, the house sat on the market with a string of estate agents for over seven years before Gandy slipped in through the backdoor like a lodger on the QT. *Peep-o! What you charging, duck?* He opened his cheque book and they were gone the next day.

No.12 was Winnie Wilson. Born in a poorhouse up Chell. All worry beads and woodbines and werriting about the weather. She was ninety-nine when she died. Stress seemed to suit her. Constance said she'd died early because she didn't want a telegram from the Queen. Didn't do posh folk did Winnie, chip on her shoulder, bunions on her feet, she'd say, "If you only make it to fifty then that's all God wanted to promise you." Longevity, it seemed, she kept all to herself.

Last but not least was No. 13. Unlucky for some and stuck on the end, it had seen seventy-three years of Constance Minton, though she told folk she'd been born in there (not true), that she'd even learnt to walk in there (not true either), that she'd accepted Ned's grandmother's thinning engagement ring in there (that was true), had been carried over the threshold by Ned into there (sort of true), Ned often saying, "You didn't marry me Connie, you married the bloody house!"

Sunday dinners and tomato plants in the summer. That's what Totty remembers most. Saturday baking and Monday morning spit and polish of the shoes. Spilt vinegar on the kitchen floor. Duck egg blue flaking off the walls. Pigeon do down the front window. Lemon juice to clean it off. Beds changed Monday. Bathroom cleaned Tuesday. Big shop Friday. Chippy tea in front of a black and white TV. Camp-beds in the parlour. Malcolm on one. Frank on the other. *They have homes, Connie. They're not our responsibility. You have your own son.* Beds changed Monday. Bathroom cleaned Tuesday. Camp-beds in the parlour. Joss on one. Kirty on the other. *We need our own place, mother. We're not your responsibility. I've been your son. Let me go and be their father.* Beds changed Monday. Bathroom cleaned Tuesday. *Don't leave me son.* Camp-beds in the parlour. *I'll die without you.* Beds changed Monday. Bathroom cleaned Tuesday. Camp-beds in the parlour. *I am proud of him Mr Povey, I have to be. But some people are just meant for the bottom of the heap.* None of it was anything to write home about, and if Ned had had his way, all those years ago, Totty would've just come to haunt the place as the little boy who never grew up. Then, on second thoughts, that's all he'd done anyway for no-one knew he was there, even now.

*

The plan was to say it out loud. "We're leaving, mother. Now." And that he wouldn't look her in the eye when he said it, because if he was at the bottom of the heap like she said, it was a long way looking up. So he would say that too. "Do you see mother, how being at the bottom of the heap means I can't look you in the eye?" And that he wasn't sorry at all.

Totty let himself in and left the door on the snip. He took a deep breath and called out. "Mother?"

Not in the kitchen. Not in the parlour. He made for the stairs. "Mother?" Not in her bedroom. Not in the bathroom. *I am proud of him Mr Povey, I have to be. But some people are just meant for the bottom of the heap.* "Connie? You in?" She had even denied him of *this*.

He went into his mother's bedroom first, and headed for the bedside drawers. A lamp sat on a woollen doily. Pink. Purple wool. An old baby cardigan of Kirty's unravelled to be of some use again. An alarm clock. Stopped at ten past seven. Its batteries out of juice. A photograph. A gold frame. Of Totty. Of the kids. Sat on the front step of Bennett Road pulling ugly faces. Totty cannot remember the occasion, or why she had chosen this picture to be what she first saw when she woke up, what she last saw before she switched off the light?

Totty picked up the photograph and looked at it. His son. His daughter. *His son. His daughter.* He could always, *always* see the resemblance. In both of them. Kirty had his eyes. She *definitely* had his eyes, that burning desire in them to be someone else. Joss. Joss had his... he had his...

Totty looked at the photograph more closely. So tall. So slim. So formed. So handsome. Even when pulling a face. He had his mother's eyes, certainly. So expressive. So responsive: you'd believe every word he said then follow him under a bus. He had that knack to make you feel like it was just, and only ever, you two. His father's anger: he'd inherited that alright. That feeling of never being in the right place, that there was never ever going to be a right time either.

He pulled the photograph from the frame and stuffed it into his overalls pocket. Then he opened the top drawer of his mother's bedside cabinet and put his hand inside feeling, as he had done for many years now, for the money his mother stashed inside distrusting of banks. And to pay for a nice mahogany coffin polished and gleaming and smelling of lavender. No carnations. Carnations were thrown at coffins by the gypsies. She wanted roses. Pink roses. And in bud. The thorns removed. The wake she wanted at the house. She could watch it all happening then. No smoking in the house. And get nice bottles of sherry. Like we have at Christmas. And play me Tom Jones. The Green Green Grass of Home. There was, Totty counted, just shy of three and a half thousand pounds.

£3,000.90p was what she'd cashed in from Ned's life insurance all those years ago and then given to Malcolm simply because he'd asked. When Totty had asked her, "How much did dad leave us?" she'd biffed him with the fish slice. "How dare you! How dare you reduce your father's life to pounds and pence." Yet the money was already spent.

Still, Gandy had given it back, like he'd promised, and there it'd stayed. In the bedside drawer. Old money now. Old notes. He would just be borrowing it. Not all of it. Just a few hundred quid to tie him over until he got himself straight. And it would be real nice for him to get in one of those KFC buckets for Sunday dinner. Kirty would love that. And they'd invite Constance over for tea, and she'd see the house and they'd all sit at the table, *his table,* and she would see, *she would see it all,* accomplishment after accomplishment, and she'd know then why he'd done it, why he'd done it all. He'd made the right decision and they would all live happily ever after because everyone would know what it was like to not live with each other all the time.

Totty took out £500. Put the rest back and shut the drawer.

Then he thought better of it.

He opened the drawer again and withdrew the lot.

He then went into his own bedroom. The room of a little boy, a small man never allowed to grow up; whatever he was out there stopped as soon as he walked in here and he had, a long time ago, stopped sleeping in here, as if that single bed had shortened him, narrowed his mind, and thinned his time. So he would sleep in the armchair instead, in the kitchen, by the stove, feigning night shifts when hungover, pretending he'd just walked in from hard graft.

He pulled out three rucksacks from under his bed that he'd been packing for some weeks. Toothbrush and pyjamas, pants, socks stuffed with cash, and a couple of changes of clothes; sentimental clothes, clothes he knew that he'd bought. Not his mother. Not Lux. Him. Then there were a few personals, stuff to remember each other by in case they got split up, and a tool. Monkey wrench in one, long handed screwdriver in the other, because a war was coming. It must be waged and they had to be vigilant. He pulled out two library cards next from his overalls pocket and added them to each rucksack. It was most important for them to be always able to get hold of a book. And waterproofs. You could never trust the weather either.

The third rucksack was more a holdall that would have to be carried by hand. This one had been packed and repacked many times with general items they would all need: toothpaste, soap, hand towels and face cloths, a six pack of crisps, a family size bar of Dairy Milk, three microwavable cottage pies and a tin of baked beans. There was a loaf. He'd recently added a slab of butter. He'd even thought to pack a knife, UHT milk, teabags, Basildon Bond notepaper, and pens. The mugs were plastic, ideal for camping, for his beer he'd swig from the can. Sleeping bags hung from each rucksack and he'd got a bag of tealights, just in case. A train timetable was stuffed in the inside pocket. The times of the buses that left the end of the street.

He checked each rucksack and tried all zips. Lifted each one to test their weight. He sat back down on the bed and gave himself a moment to feel something. *I am proud of him Mr Povey, I have to be. But some people are just meant for the bottom of the heap.*

Nothing came.

Feel something, he urged. Feel it, *feel it now!*

His bedroom door opened. "Now?" It was Kirty with a gaping stare. "Mr Gandy wants us to go right now?"

Totty looked at his daughter and saw Joss standing behind her. Both were wearing their coats.

"You know he's cut the power," Joss told his father, flicking the hallway light switch up and down. "He didn't have to cut the power on her. That's just mean."

"He's making his point," Totty replied. "He's making sure I stick to our agreement."

Joss looked down at the rucksacks and tapped at each one with his foot. "And she fell," he told his dad. "She was trying to change the batteries in the kitchen clock. She came off the step ladder. We found her on the kitchen floor."

Totty pursed his lips. "She got up though?"

"Yeah, we got her up."

Joss watched his father struggle to lift even the smaller of the rucksacks and attach it to Kirty's back. She complained. The straps were too tight. It was heavier than last time. He'd probably packed all the wrong things again. She wanted her poncho and if she was going to be a snail and wear her house on her back then she wanted her teeny-boppers – her 'ten-eyes' as she called them – and her swimming goggles - her x-ray specs – to see things in cupboards before they saw her. She pulled the rucksack away from her, dumped it on the landing and folded her arms.

"I'm not going," she said, stamping her foot.

Totty shrugged at her. "Then we'll just go without you."

Kirty seemed to find this funny. "Doesn't matter if you do," she said, pulling a set of keys from her trouser pocket and dangling them in front of her dad. "I'm not even locked out."

"Where did you get these?" and Totty snatched them from her hand.

She looked guilty. "Kitchen table," she said quietly.

Totty looked at the little plastic nametag attached to the set of the keys. He closed his eyes. He didn't need to be able to spell to know how Gandy worked. He'd given Constance keys so even if Totty and the kids left, she'd still be able to let herself in. Wherever he went, she would always, always have a key.

"We have to go," he said earnestly, and unzipped the bottom pocket of Kirty's rucksack. "Ten eyes," he said smiling, handing her the teeny-boppers. "And x-ray specs." He put them on for her and kissed her forehead. "We really have to go now though, right?" But she looked up at Joss for her answer.

He was still staring at his dad, wondering for the stains on his overalls, the blood caked about his wrist. "Look at the state of you," Joss murmured. "You look like you've been on a bender then scrapping in the chippy with a fat bird who's left teeth marks."

Totty glowered behind the pile of rucksacks. "Just get your bag, gutter-gob, and let's go."

Joss looked down at the rucksacks. Another bag packed. Another place to go. "Maybe we should just wait," he said. "Till Nan gets back. Then we can talk to her. *I'll* talk to her. We'll tell her, properly. We can't go like this."

"And maybe we should think about why we're doing this," Totty's eyes gesturing towards Kirty who was muttering into her swimming goggles. "Maybe we need to remember how much time we don't have."

"We're only doing this because Gandy wants this house and you've given in to him."

"We're doing this Joss, because I want you to have a future. *Your* future. That's something I've never had."

"But I don't need to leave here to have it."

"Yes you do. Believe me. You do."

Joss stepped away from the rucksacks and began making his way down the stairs. "I've been covering for you all week," he shouted back. "I'm sick of pretending it doesn't matter."

Totty clambered over the rucksacks to follow his son down the stairs. "You can handle it," he told him as Joss reached the hallway and spun round to tell his dad, "I have handled it."

"As I knew you would."

"But we don't know where she is. We were about to go looking for her."

"Then we don't have much time," said Totty, heading back up the stairs. He dragged the three rucksacks to the top of the landing then let them slide down the steps, each one thudding atop of the other, instructing Joss to take that rucksack, that's the heaviest, that's yours, strapping the other rucksack to Kirty again as she frowned and whimpered. She did not want to be an adventurer today. Or a snail. People trod on snails and killed them without a care for the fact that they've just squished their body *and* their home. They think it doesn't hurt them because they're squidgy and have no bones, but it does. I know it does. "And then they're homeless!" Kirty wailed. "And they can't just build another shell so everyone, in the whole world, can see them hurt and pathetic and all on their own!"

Totty pushed the front door open wide and told them both to get out of the house. "Go on," he said. "Both of you. Out! Now!"

He slammed the door shut behind him and then pushed his keys through the letterbox. He pointed down the street and told his kids, "I promise. This time, this time it'll be good." And though they followed, neither of them believed him.

Round 36

When Gandy had first shown Totty around Fairview earlier in the week, he had kept asking, "what's the catch?"

No catch, he was assured, just a big, open comprehensive offer, call it a partnership if he liked. "Of course, we're just talking, talking," Gandy had added. "Partnerships need contracts and I've some things I want you to bear in mind before we put this to bed," and Totty had lit Gandy's cigarette and poached one from the pack.

It was a grand house was Fairview, bloody grand, every item of furniture so brand spanking new it was yet to be unleashed of its plastic or price tag. Everything fitted, everything suited, and everything had been built for three: three beds, three-seater sofa, three leather backed stools, three chairs, three bean-bags, three cushions, and, "Three bedrooms," Gandy kept repeating. "Three fucking bedrooms, comrade." And then, in case Totty still hadn't believed him. "There they are. Three fucking bedrooms."

The curtains draped. The porridge was still warm, and Totty ran his fingers across the fabrics like a wife. "But no bay windows," he pointed out.

"You have to work for a bay, comrade," Gandy replied. "This place punches well above your standing as it is." And he began to tell him a tale about a mate who knew boilers, the very latest in energy-saving models. It'd be fitted up in the loft, he said, out of sight, warm as toast, freeing up the airing cupboard to extend the bathroom. "Think about it comrade. A free-standing bath, taps in the middle, a lady misbehaving in the bubbles."

It was a lovely thought and Totty was nuts to think otherwise.

"I know you value honesty, comrade," Gandy had pressed on, leading Totty in and out of the three bedrooms, one pink, one straw, the last a woody looking apricot with fitted wardrobes. "So this place lets you hide in plain sight." Totty had frowned in agreement.

"As for Connie, I've just the place for her," and they were back downstairs and heading into a smallish room with a low ceiling and exposed brickwork. It was once the garage then renovated by the previous owners for a dilapidated parent who bumped into the furniture and apologised to it. "Of course, I've talked to Connie about the bungalows," Gandy carried on, as he opened a door to showcase a walk-in closet, coat-hangers clanging for clothes. "Thought it best I get that in her mind before she cops a load of this place and moves in before you," and he play-punched Totty between the shoulder blades.

"You know you're out of your fucking mind to think I'll take this," Totty had told him, walking around the room, taking it all in, choking upon the lot.

"It's a question of etiquette, comrade," Gandy had said. "I'm just covering all angles."

"From your point of view."

"And you should do your children a very big favour and see this place from *their* point of view."

"I don't want it."

"You know that's not an option."

"I could walk into a cop-shop right now and tell them what I saw."

"And you know very well that men like you work for men like me. They'd never believe you."

"What I saw was the fucking truth."

"And there you go again, comrade. Longing for what you can't see anymore," and he'd put his arm around Totty and given him a squeeze. "They always say that a dog is the most faithful friend you'll ever have," he'd began. "So you can see this one of two ways comrade. This is a free good home, or you're guarding my property. I'll leave it to you to see it as you will."

Totty swatted his arm away. "Do you know how fucking insulting you are?"

"You used to be able to charm the hind legs off a no-smoking sign," Gandy had chided. "Game as a badger, as I remember."

"And you got away with bloody murder as I remember."

"No, accidents happen, comrade, and then only some of us get away with murder."

Totty had stood in front of Gandy until the gap between them was about six inches in old money on the tape measure. "Oh come on now, Totty lad." It was always Gandy to speak first. "It's far better for it to happen before she goes so that the kids come to know a house without her," and he'd looked Totty straight in the eye. "See-saws, comrade, some of us go up, some of us go down, that's just fucking life."

"A plague on every one of your fucking houses," because Totty was seething.

Gandy frowned. "Shakespeare, comrade?" he'd mocked. "Getting a little ahead of yourself, aren't you? Best I bring you down a peg or two," and he'd laughed manically before ordering Totty to take another good look around. "Then pull the door hard on your way out," he'd instructed. "You'll be last in so first accused," and the laughing had rung in Totty's ears for days.

But when Totty turned the key in the front door of Fairview with his children in tow, the house felt cold, real cold. Cold enough to make your teeth chatter and your lungs ache. The power was off. The place was empty, the whole lot gone. Everything. Stripped back to the bare floorboards and even the light bulbs had been removed. He felt stupid saying dining room, front room, kitchen and stairs. Totty rushed his children up the stairs thinking maybe, just maybe, there was a heart still beating in Gandy somewhere, but he'd even swindled the children.

"Really?" said Joss. "This is what you agreed?"

"You got your fucking bedroom didn't you?" and Totty forgot

himself in the disappointment. "I didn't mean that," fumbling an apology, but Joss was beginning to simmer.

"Don't pin this on me," he began. "You're the father here. Provide. Like all the other dads do. Stand on a soggy wet football pitch Sunday morning and make me think I'm man of the match."

But Totty was gone. He was in the next door bedroom bullshitting Kirty about how sunny her room was.

"You can draw anything you like on the walls Kirty. I'll buy you some proper felt tips tomorrow, you know, the ones that never come off?"

She looked down at the floorboards. "What will I draw daddy?" she asked.

"Everything," he said. "And anything you like."

"But I can't draw furniture," she said solemnly. "It's too hard."

The price list was easy to find. It'd been typed out, printed off a computer on headed paper and Blu-tacked to a kitchen cupboard door. Each piece of furniture was accounted for right down to the stainless steel utensils that'd hung next to the hob, though that wasn't there either. That too would have to be earned.

Gandy said that he'd made everything as clear as possible, that each job Totty undertook would be paid in furniture and buy him time - electric, gas, water - it was all about buying minutes for this and trading minutes for that. You've got to learn, comrade. This life don't come for free. Much of it was written in capital letters, perhaps in the hope that Totty might be able to read it for himself, or because Gandy knew how degrading it'd be for Totty to have to hear the terms of their partnership read out aloud to him by his son.

As Joss read, Totty sank to his knees, the weight of his rucksack just too much to bear. Joss stopped reading. He read the rest of the terms in silence then stuck the list back where he'd found it with chewed gum. He made no attempt to console his father. Instead, he watched Kirty kneel down aside of him, one goggle over her left eye, and her headlamp still on full beam. She said, "Pieces of eight daddy, don't cry. All pirates find the treasure in the end." But Totty had nothing left to give.

*

Totty's mobile phone rang a fourth time. That'd be right, he thought seeing no number on the screen. Call from a phone box. Not own up. Typical Constance when she knew she was in the wrong. *I am proud of him Mr Povey, I have to be. But some people are just meant for the bottom of the heap.* But you hurt my feelings, son, Constance would retort. You've wounded me.

He left the phone on top of the toilet cistern in the end, cleaning his teeth by a tea-light. There was no mirror on the wall to spit at. No hot water to scald his face. He padded down the stairs as quietly as he could given the bare floorboards and nicked his left foot on an upturned screw. It drew blood. He made no attempt to mop it up.

He went into the living room where Joss and Kirty had made a pirate camp with their sleeping bags, rucksacks for pillows, both still wearing yesterday's clothes. They left tea-lights burning on the hearth because passing ships saw fires, Kirty had insisted. They would be rescued by morning she was sure.

"Do you think Nan's alright by herself?" Kirty tried to stay awake. "She's never lived in the house all on her own."

"She'll have the big lights on," Joss whispered. "And granddad's angel is in the walls of course. He won't let anything bad happen. You know that," and he started to hum. A hard day's night. Not because it was a lullaby. But because it's what Totty used to sing to them as babies. It's been a hard day's night. You should be sleeping like a log.

Once Kirty was asleep, Joss told the small dark hump to his left side, "I could quit school. We'd get things done quicker then. Make it a proper home."

But the small dark hump to his left side said no.

No.

No.

You get them exams done then you get the fuck away and you take her with you.

Round 37

"What are you doing with my wallet son?"

"Just looking."

"There's nowt in it."

"Is this you?"

"Not now, eh son? It's one o'clock in the morning. Get some shut-eye, eh?"

"How old are you here in this picture?"

"About three. Scrawny little nipper weren't I? Wouldn't say boo to a goose. That's yer Nan. Me dad's behind the camera. See how she holds me? See how she won't let go?"

"She will be alright, won't she?"

"Give me that. Let me show you properly. Come on. You want a can? *Tshh.* Come on. Have a drink with yer old man. It's Saturday night. In days gone by you'd be supping at the bar with me. Here. Cheers. Let me look at these properly. Crikey. I didn't know I'd got half of these. What am I here? Seven? Eight? That's Malcolm. And that's not his bike. He took lots of things that weren't his, even then. Used to give us a backy to school. Never let us ride it. Said I didn't know how. He had a brother once, you know, leukaemia. Don't know how old. His mother never got over it. Took to the drink, wandering the streets. Yer Nan used to go out to her, *Come on now Elsa, let's me and you go have a fag and a talk,* she was the only one who ever got through to her. We found his brother's wheelchair stashed up his dad's allotment in the shed. Used it like a go-kart. Pick up some real speed with a good run up. Though I never got my run up right. Nothing ever right according to Malcolm. But he called for me. He came knocking for me. His dad had said to him, *Go find some lads your own age. Go play with them.* Because he had this thing, did Mally, for older lads, you know? Used to follow this one bloke because he was the only one on his street who went to work in a suit. Turned out he worked for some posh hotel. What do you call them, those that stand about waiting for luggage? Anyway, he was one of them. That was all. But Malcolm, he followed him everywhere. *See him? I'll have a suit like that one day,* and Frank would be laughing his head off. He knew it was never just about a nice bloody suit.

"Christ, I'd forgotten this one was in here. Look at us. Bloody filthy we were. Frank was so dirt poor he only ever had a bath once a week - got in the water after everyone else. I'm serious! Old fashioned poor I'm talking. Like days gone by. His mam in it first, then his sister, then his dad. They just never had nothing. His old man, he'd be doing this one week, doing summat else the next, and his mam would be on the settee ailing for summat else when it was the old man with the vertigo. Gunner in Korea, he was, two perforated eardrums. Had no balance after that. Used to keep buckets on the stairs for when he went up, he'd be that sick. His sister was out of there as soon as she turned seventeen. She went to Australia: fat as butter, stack of kids, never writes. God, look at us. Look at those shirt collars. Poke yer eye out with one of them.

"That's Jonty. That one there. Lanky streak of piss he was. Ate like a fucking horse. Couldn't kick a ball save his life but he had stuff, you know? Not a kid with everything but more than the rest of us. Wouldn't have known it. He was just decent. Slip yer his pocket money for a bag of chips, that sort of thing. Malcolm said he could shove his money, but he still took it. He'd take it off me. Take it off Frank. Selfish prick all his life.

"There's yer granddad. Look at him in his shirt and tie and his sleeves rolled up. That were him all over. He'd have scrubbed his hands raw before he sat down to eat, used to go at them with a wire brush. Yer Nan wouldn't have 'em anywhere near her. Murderer's hands, she called 'em. No fingerprints. And yer couldn't love him. He wouldn't let yer. Don't even know what he ever wanted for me. Pit-prop, pot-bank, or factory line. *They're all a decent wage lad. Enough for a man like you.* He knew I were nuthin like him from the moment he clapped eyes on me. Had to really force himself, you know, and I'm not sure he even did that. Funny thing bringing up another man's son. Oh, I knew he weren't me dad for a long time. Even before he said and told me who probably was. But it never really bothered me. Dunna know why. Guess I knew I was always going be a disappointment, so since yer granddad was always bloody disappointed, I just stuck it out with him. Though I still hoped. Yer can see it in me face. All that hope. Photos always give yer away.

"Of course, I went to fetch him the day Jonty fell. Thought he'd see me being a hero, you know, raising the alarm. But I couldn't find him. Wasn't on shift. Day off, they said down on Minton's, and yer granddad never took a day off in his life. Still don't know where he was, he never, ever said, and yet I looked bloody everywhere. Kept going. Kept looking. He were the only person I wanted to find. But I can keep on looking for the rest of my life and I won't ever find the bastard. Some folk, if they can't get lost, disappear for good.

"Your mother. I used to love this picture of her. Look at her. She's a one. Beautiful. Really bloody beautiful. Been trouble, caused trouble, and not bloody worth the trouble either. I have loved your mum Joss, more than you'll ever understand. Because she's for me and I'm for her and one day we'll get it right, but it anna going be anytime soon son. I grant yer that. She just wants too much.

"This? I keep this because it's the only bloody thing I have official with my name on it. Just a library card I know, but still. You're nowt in this life without a name and yer Nan even changed that to keep me and have people think of me what they do. That's why I keep it son. I might not read the books but you can tell an awful lot by just looking at the pictures. Then and now, son. *Then and now.* You canna get your head round it what they've done to this place. Take the pot out the potteries and what have yer got? Just the trees son. Just the trees. And they'll chop all them down for a new estate.

"What's this? You know this. You've got a piece yourself. This is because I like being on my own. House full of family. Thousands at work. Hundreds on the streets. All of you going for the same job, sitting at the same tables down the Tanners, supping from yesterday's pints, stood in the same queues, obeying a thousand rules and a hundred laws: I can't get away quick enough sometimes. So that's why me, you, and Kirty have a bit of this plate each. So when I want to be on my own and get away I've got this to remind me that we're still in it together.

"You see, the way I see it is that I was meant for a world already on its way out. Runts like me son, we're never going to get all these computers and qualifications and whatever else the government thinks is going to get us off the dole. You could be this. You could be that. I was born for summat and I'll die for nowt because this new world don't need men like me. Robot does it faster. Computer don't need paying. Neither answer back or will join a fucking union. But they dunna have our pride. Our devotion. Our trust. Flip a plate over son and you'll see none of them have been baked with any love.

"But you got a brain lad. It ain't from me, that's for sure, but you got one, and you should use it and be grateful for it, because you canna get by in this bloody world thick as two short planks.

"No. Don't. I know what I am. And I know what folk think an' all. Think folk like me should just pull our finger out, stop scabbing and get to fucking work. Well, we would if we could. We aren't that fucking choosy. Take owt. But if there's nowt doing and you're up against another thirty or so men, it starts to peeve. You end up thinking sod it. And then you start on the pills cheer you up. Don't fucking touch the sides with me. Start wondering if anything's going to help you, if anyone's going to give you a hand. Because you can't rely on yer mates like yer used to. Stab yer in the back then use yer as a shield, save their own life first then go back to your gaff and get their feet under the table with yer old dear. Fucking Frank. He thinks I don't know. He thinks I've no bloody idea what designs he's got on all of you. Thinks I've got it all whilst Gandy keeps trying to take it all. Well, I tell yer what son....

"Look at that. One can of lager and he sleeps. Like everyone else, eh Joss? Not even you will listen to a word I've got to say."

Round 38

Early Sunday morning with the sun barely dressed: Totty took a leak and listened to his mobile phone ringing in his pocket. Still calling from phone boxes. Still trying to have it her way. This was the longest that he and Constance had gone without speaking and yet this was the time when there was so much to say. Well, he'd had enough. Old tricks. New numbers. Got that social worker on her side now. Ganging up. So he chucked the phone down the toilet and flushed. Now no-one could reach them. They were finally on their own.

He opened the bathroom door.

"We can't live like this."

"Can I get out of the bog first?"

"It's not fair on Kirt."

"Don't you think I know that, Joss?"

"Then what are you going to do about it? Because if the social get wind of what this place looks like, or if mum finds out where we are with no furniture, we'll be back with her like a shot," and Joss clicked his fingers in his father's face.

"But I got custody," Totty explained. "I won you in a court of law."

"You don't win children, dad," Joss began, exasperated, as Kirty called out from downstairs to *watch me!* She was cart-wheeling from one room to the next. *Thirty-two. Thirty-three.* The dizzying sound of feet hitting floorboards. *Thirty-four. Thirty-five. Daddy, you're not watching me! Thirty-six. Thirty-seven. Daddy, it's a new world record!*

Totty and Joss went down the stairs to watch. Joss picked up the count for her. "Thirty-eight, thirty-nine, forty! And the gold medal goes to Kirty Minton of Great Britain!" He made the relevant noises for a crowd's thunderous applause and stamped his feet as his sister took a bow and waved at the crowd. She punched the air and shouted, "Daddy, daddy! Did you see me? Did you see me do them all without stopping? Did you see how straight my legs were?"

"Yes," Totty lied. "I saw every single one."

Joss looked his father. "But that's just the thing. You never see or see anything through. Like you used to hand us over to mum in Morrison's car-park when you'd run out of money."

Totty grabbed hold of his son by his T-shirt and shoved him up against the wall of the front room. His right forearm pinned him against it and his boot-clad feet stepped on Joss' toes. Kirty screamed.

"No daddy! No!"

But treat as you wished to be treated, Totty always said. And if you were man enough to speak to your own father like that then you were man enough to defend your words.

"You want me to feel guilty?" Totty spat. "You want me to feel anymore shitty than I already do? Because I know I was born a fucking dud son, but I don't need you to tell me that. Do you understand?" And then with a finger pointed in his face, "*Do you understand?*"

What Joss did understand was that he was the stronger of the two. That if push came to shoving and punching his dad would not come out of it particularly well. So he told him very gently that, "We can't be kept children forever, dad. Even I can see what that does to a man. Do you understand *me*?"

At the time, Totty hadn't, not quite. Or perhaps he did and just didn't want to hear it. And it was, as he might have to plead, a moment of temporary madness that lifted his fist and pushed it towards his son's kidneys. The second punch Joss took for his grandmother; it'd been delivered with such venom. The third because he didn't want to fight back. It wasn't a matter of respect. It was a matter of picking on someone your own size. He didn't go down either. The punches were lightweight. Perhaps they were meant to be. But Joss grabbed his father's fourth fist before it connected. He looked down at Totty's withered clenched hand and said, "This is why we'd better off without you," whilst Kirty, at her brother's side, kicked her father in the shin and said, "We have all these rooms daddy, and you never watched me cartwheel in them once."

At that, Joss pulled his father towards their rucksacks, Totty limp as a ragdoll, his feet barely skimming the floorboards. There was something he needed to see. "You're not the only one so fucking angry out there," Joss shouted. "Like it shouldn't matter where we live," now throwing him onto the floor in a heap. "As long as you come home that's all that matters to me and her." And then something else was thrown - something white and plastic and hard - it hit the back of Totty's head and burst apart.

Coppers, dog-ends, and buttons. A lost earring, a daisy-chain of paperclips, half a snapped key, a raffle ticket. Kirby grips, a Durex wrapper, a few more pence, a little silver, a lot of fluff, a half-sucked polo mint, but no gold: the charity pot contained more bric-a-brac worth even less than the couple of quid that scattered about the living room floor; Kirty darting in between their legs to catch the rolling pennies before they landed, like a cat chasing balls of string. So that's what people gave to enable other people to live a little better, Joss thought, whilst his father looked down at the floor.

"I have no idea why I did it," Joss kneeling in front of his dad now, his eyes reddening with the shame. "Because what sort of person nicks a charity pot? It wasn't even worth it. Didn't even get reported for doing it."

Totty reached out to him. "But you're different," he began.

"No I'm not," and Joss rubbed at his nose hard. "I can't be. I'd never fucking survive round here if I was."

Totty pulled himself up onto his knees. "Yer granddad used to say that two suns rose every morning round here. One for us lot and then one for everyone else. Difference being everyone else was on the beach." He reached for his tobacco pouch. "You could be sat in a deckchair with them too, son. That's why it doesn't matter."

"It does matter!" and Joss was raging. "Why aren't you angry? Why have we always got to be so fucking gracious in accepting everybody's charity because you can't do it?"

Because it'd been a life of hand-me-down this and second-hand that. *You say thank you to the nice lady now Jossy. Tell the man how kind.* And he'd extend a small hand to say thank you. For what I have received, I should be truly thankful - for coppers and dog-ends, buttons and paperclip chains, for Kirby grips, and a whole lot of fluff - Joss had learnt very early on not to insult the nice lady and the contents of her charity pots.

Joss looked down at his dad sat on the bare floorboards chuffing on his roll-up. He had watched his father potter through his life and occasionally drop by his, and he'd known for some time now that if he didn't knuckle down it'd be a life just like his dad's - one charity pot to the next - coppers, dog-ends, and buttons, a few more pence but never any gold.

"All I ever do is for you," Totty murmured at the floorboards."Even when I'm not here, I'm out there doing for you."

"Out there? Out there? Well, let me tell you about out there," and Joss was striding, his arms swinging at his side. "Let me tell you how I can barter with a smack-head over whether you get more for your money if you shop in metric and not imperial, but no-one can help me with the fractions in my maths homework because that makes me a swot."

"Don't be a smart-arse," Totty smiled. "You want to get out of the toilet then you pull yourself out. No-one can do it for you Joss. Not even me."

"And your life isn't as shit as you keep making out," Joss replied. "You're just fucking bone idle." But he only had the courage to walk out of the room into another room, because leaving the house completely would definitely confirm that he was his mother's son after all.

*

Kirty's right palm was splayed and littered with black dots. "Funeral director," she went. "I've got another dead one for you."

"Stick them in here." Joss pointed at the flower pot they'd been filling with soil and lining with dead leaves having hunted out what Kirty had called, "the crippled, sick and the dead," preparing a mass grave. She was wearing her granddad's trilby, his old reading glasses with the lenses pushed out, and she crawled about Fairview's garden on all fours with her magnifying glass looking for signs of death.

"And then after we've sung the hymns we'll go home and see Nan," Kirty said.

Joss patted the soil down with his hand before looking up at the back of the house. He was just able to catch sight of his father's shadow watching them both from the bedroom window.

"You do know why we have to live here, don't you?" he said quietly, his sister humming All Things Bright and Beautiful, being her Nan's favourite hymn and the only one Kirty knew. She nodded her head. "So you do know that going to see Nan is not going home anymore. We live here now, and Nan can come and see us, *here*, at our home," as if repeating the words would convince him too.

Kirty looked up at her brother through her granddad's reading glasses. Even without the lenses her eyes seemed too big for her face. "It's just been a very long time already," she said under her breath.

"Not really," Joss tried to explain. "It's just been one sleep. And we live here now," closing his eyes, knowing what he had to do, understanding that his childhood was ever so long ago. "She can come and see us when she's ready."

"But she went off with that man without telling us."

"No, the man drove away in his van. Nan went somewhere else."

"Where?"

He looked up at the bedroom window again whilst he thought about what to say.

"You do know Kirty that one day Nan will go somewhere without telling us and won't come back at all?" He cleared his throat a little after he'd said it, watching his little sister blink behind the glasses. "I know that will make you very sad," he pressed on. "And I'll be sad too. But if we don't see her every day." He stopped. He looked down at the flower pot. At all the crippled, sick, and the dead.

Kirty leant towards him and ruffled his hair. "Everybody dies Joss," she said light-heartedly. "It's not the end of the world when you're just going to a better one." And she jumped up from the paving slabs, stuck both hands in the air, and shouted at the lawn, "Ladies and gentlemen! Boys and girls. Prepared to be thrilled as Kirty Minton cartwheels for gold for Great Britain!"

Totty counted thirty-two consecutive cartwheels from the bedroom window before he couldn't count anymore and had to turn away, but Joss didn't count a single one.

*

Watching his children play was something that Totty did but never let on that he was. Up at the bedroom window, the double-glazing made it difficult for him to hear them properly, but what he picked up through lip-reading had made his heart thump. His knees buckled several times before he finally gave in and gripped onto the window sill. All those things he kept promising: he'd failed them again. Brought them to a shell where they could see for themselves just how hard he was prepared to work, what it was he was doing 'out there' when he said he was 'out there'. He wouldn't just have to graft but would have that graft monitored, by Gandy, by his mother, by his kids. Everyone would be able to see just how hard Totty Minton was prepared to work. It was humiliating. And he felt hurt and pathetic and all on his own.

But there was still a choice. He could suffer it or go begging. And he could still do that. He could still bring himself to do that. Frank could be a real soft touch at times.

He moved away from the window after watching Kirty say a little prayer, her hands neatly pressed together and pointing towards the sky. He padded down the stairs, manacled himself back to the toolbox with the toilet chain, took a deep breath, and left the house to finish all he'd tried to start.

Sunday 9th May
2010

Round 39

After the fall, Lux had run to Constance not because she cared, but because she could see that there was something in it for her. So she did a fair amount of wailing and shrieked instructions. *This is my children's grandmother. She's a true potter. Honour her. Help her. For fuck's sake. Someone call 999.* Folk afraid to pull out their mobile phones in an area renown for snatching.

But Lux was also suspicious. Constance was not only running about the precinct without her coat, headscarf, and shopping truck, but wearing her slippers and showing a little petticoat. She carried no bag and looked as if she'd been giving chase or being pursued: either way it was a funny business, and Lux at least spared Constance the indignity of having her petticoat round her knees by covering her damaged legs with her jacket.

Lux did more wailing in the ambulance. Wailed a little more when they got to A&E. It was, she had to admit, a heck of a performance and she'd begun to wonder whether she actually cared after all. Because,

Constance MINTON	versus	Lux FAITHFUL
You're too young for him.		Grow up Connie.
You're just a kid.		Let him go.
You're too selfish to have kids.		You keep him a baby.
You preyed on him.		You suffocate him. He can't breathe.
He could do so much better.		So could I. *I do.*
You love money.		You love control.
I don't know what you're doing with him.		You've brainwashed him.

We have no money to give you.	Oh here we go.
You can't hold down a job.	And then turn on the tears.
You want to be kept.	He's not yours to keep.
You don't like work.	There is nothing for us here.
You're idle.	You're evil.
You're devious, a liar.	Pot. Kettle. Black.
But you like to spend. Other people's money.	It's all other people's money.
You do nothing for those kids.	You don't let me.
You don't know how to be a mother.	I'll always be their mother.
Kids come so easily to the wrong people.	And kids have to grow up.
Why don't you just bugger off and leave?	I keep trying.
It's all you ever do anyway.	Why do you always have to have the last word?
I don't.	How are you so content with nothing, Connie? Being such a nothing with nothing to leave behind?
	What's up Connie? Cat got your tongue?

Constance Minton was now nothing more than another old woman lying dying in a bed next to another old woman lying dying in a bed on a hospital ward where old women came to die. She'd been brought here by ambulance with just the clothes on her back, and which had been handed to Lux who shoved them into a Morrison's carrier bag intending to find a bin for them on her way out. Or she might set fire to them, she hadn't made her mind up yet, because cremation, Constance always said, was for witches.

Lux had filled in some forms on their arrival, doctoring telephone numbers, making up the rest, and she put herself as the distressed next of kin. All the while she wrote she wept. She'd apologised to the ward sister for the dampness of the forms. The ward sister had offered her tea and biscuits and found her a comfy armchair which she'd had dragged to the side of Constance's bed by an overweight porter with a lot to do. And there Lux had spent the night underneath a scratchy blanket that made her nose itch. Every now and then she'd nip out into the night air for a fag and a chat with the paramedics awaiting their next emergency call. With one she even exchanged numbers.

By morning, she was informed by a change of staff that the registrar would be round to put her in the picture. She was warned that things weren't looking good. Other than a change of stoma and a shift in pillows, Constance hadn't stirred. It was an induced coma, they said. The stroke had commandeered her right side completely and the next forty-eight hours were crucial. A machine beeped and occasionally cut out. A hospital trolley dawdled past offering tea, a little something to eat, but no, Lux said, finding more tears. She couldn't possibly eat a thing when she was *this* upset, then she pulled the curtains around the bed and sat back down.

Except the curtain was immediately pulled back by a clumsy hand. The lady in the next bed was crying. "I don't know what to do," she sobbed. "I don't know what to do. You'll have to tell me what to do."

"There's nothing to do," Lux told the woman. "And nothing you can do about it either."

Then, the curtain behind her armchair was pulled by the other lady in the bed to the right. "Can't you pull these back?" she asked Lux. "I can't see anything with these curtains pulled across like this. I'm all claustrophobic, and if they can't see me they'll forget me. I could die behind here and no-one would ever know."

Lux got up from the chair and padded softly towards the curtain. "It won't be long now," she said, taking command of the curtain. "Not long. I promise," and she pulled the curtain further around Constance's bed and returned to her seat with an overwhelming sense of relief.

Round 40

Frank Blatch, in casual clothes, had come to see Maggie Gifford with a bribe. He had also purchased a bouquet of chrysanthemums from the petrol station that stunk of screen-wash, and had both rung the bell and flipped her letterbox for some time. He'd peered through the front window and then gone round the back of the house because something was wrong. He could smell it. By the time he'd got to the backdoor he had known that if he didn't kick it down he'd be too late. He'd run at the door with his most powerful boot and the door had swung open.

He smelt gas.

He expected her to be on the floor flat-out, God forbid, dead, and he assumed that she wouldn't thank him for saving her life when she'd been leaving for donkeys and just improving her excuses each time. But she was just sat at the kitchen table half-cut and pouring out another glass of wine; one of the gas-burners blaring behind her as she welded a can of baked beans to the pan.

Frank was far more embarrassed than Maggie was. She put the flowers in a large jug and told him they were beautiful. She wasn't keen on chrysanthemums - they reminded her of her bridal bouquet - but it'd been a long time since a man had booted down her backdoor bearing flowers and she'd found the whole thing rather racy.

She offered him a drink. He asked for tea. She looked disappointed. Whilst she lumbered about wearing yesterday's washing, Frank looked about her kitchen: a splitting headache of a room with the bad lighting of a service station and nothing looked at all at home. As she struggled to remember where she kept the milk, Frank asked, "Why do you stay here Maggie? What is it that makes you stick around in a place that shits on you from such a great height?"

She laughed. Told him that everywhere shits on you. It wasn't personal. There were no cases of favouritism in a place like this, and there were people further down the food chain than she was. "And my son's shitting on them enough so what goes around comes around," and she cheered having found teabags.

"What about your life, Maggie?" Frank asked. "Don't you want to have one?"

She didn't laugh at that. In fact, she looked peeved to be asked. She said, "The physical stuff, I can handle. The bruises rub off. The cuts close up. But the mental bits, when Jason gets right inside my head: I really struggle with that. It makes me not want anything at all." She poured hot water into a mug, dunked in a teabag at the last minute. "He was three weeks into his stretch when they called me up to tell me he'd gone on a hunger strike and they wanted my permission to feed him intravenously," she said of Jason's time in a juvenile detention centre up in the North West, whilst handing Frank a mug of tea with what drool of milk she'd found. "They said 'he'll starve otherwise' and I said, 'Yes. I suppose he will.' They had to call his father in the end. I just kept hoping he would do it."

But Frank couldn't summon any sympathy. He knew only too well how the years could pass by in a blur of comfort eating and drinking alone, as he knew that Jason, though both on bail and under curfew, was still patrolling the streets pushing his wares and thumping lumps out of his mother when he got home. Payback he called it, for she'd shopped him for dealing then stood aside when he'd got sent down – "As a message to all buyers who think this is purely recreational" - had said the judge. Frank now wondered how much the wine took the punches for her, if her kitchen bred actual vermin, where her son was patrolling right now.

"Aren't you afraid for what he might to do?" Frank asked, as Maggie fumbled about her cupboards for a biscuit tin ("I do have one. I know I have one. I used to have one anyway.")

"Of course I was afraid." She slammed a cupboard door shut. "He held a fucking hammer to my head."

She was talking about Totty. He'd been talking about Jason.

He said, "Jason would still be inside if you hadn't kept changing your statements. And here we are again Maggie. You're doing it again."

"Are you asking me *not* to press charges?"

"You don't ever press charges against Jason for what he does to you."

"That's different. He's my son."

"We're all someone's child Maggie."

"And that's the way authority goes now? A jug of flowers and please don't press any charges because they're some mother's son?"

Frank sighed. Traffic was his thing, not women, and he knew only too well what happened when a car met a woman who drank. He said, "Sometimes you want to do more than just help, especially when there's young kiddies involved."

"You do what is asked of you when your life is in danger," she replied.

"Believe me," Frank assured her. "You were in no danger."

"So you do know him."

"Only as well as I know your son, as you might know my wife," and he waited for her response.

"Your wife?"

"Yes," said Frank. "I had a wife."

"You *had* a wife?"

"Yes," said Frank. "I did. And you took her away."

"What?"

He repeated himself slowly. "I had a wife and you took her away."

"What do you mean I took her away?"

And so he said it again. "I had a wife and you took her away."

"You can keep on saying that as much as you like, but I don't know what you're telling me or what you think I know."

"You were drunk and you were driving and she was crossing the road to buy milk."

"What? When?"

"You were drunk and you were driving and she was crossing the road to buy milk."

"I still don't know what you're saying to me."

"Then I'll say it again and again until you do. You were drunk and you were driving and she was crossing the road to buy milk. You were drunk and you were driving and she was crossing the road to buy milk. You were drunk and you were driving and she was crossing the road to buy milk…"

*

It was five years to the day that Maggie had caught Frank's wife head-on as she stepped into the road to cross. The impact had killed her instantly. Maggie was going a little over 50mph in a 30mph zone and had swerved to avoid her but hit her anyway; Maggie too inebriated to apply good judgement to the width of her car. She'd hit and run so quickly that bystanders barely had the time to catch their breaths let alone jot down the registration plate, which Frank later found registered to a 1998 Vauxhall Astra bought in Nantwich. Then, he'd checked the footage from the CCTV above the chip shop, seen who was driving, but also seen who was stood on the other side of the road blotto and distracting Maggie, as he danced to the tune of the little green man at the crossing. Frank had removed the camera film, taken it home, and watched it over and over and over until the print on the rewind button rubbed off.

"If I burn this," Frank now told Maggie, and showing her the spool of tape. "Then it clears you both completely. Neither of you were ever there."

She stared at the small black box with tape spilling out as if it were about to detonate there and then. She muttered, "How long have I got?"

To which Frank told her calmly, "I think you've suffered enough."

It's like tit for tat, he explained. He hadn't pressed charges then. It'd be good if she didn't now. And then, just in case, there's twenty grand on the table. Go and get yourself a nice bit of life for once, because the one that you've got is revolting.

Maggie regarded the envelope of money as something that also might blow up in her face. She looked up at Frank, her right forefinger stretched out and grazing the tip of one of the many notes. She had never seen that much money in the flesh before. She was surprised for how papery it looked, how meaningless; like it wouldn't buy a loaf of bread. She wondered what a traffic cop was doing with that sort of cash.

Frank cleared his throat to speak. "I wanted you to know what it's like not to have the one person you really want yet have really let down," he said. "But you've suffered enough now. And so have I."

All the while he spoke, Maggie tried desperately to remember. Had she really knocked down a woman and then blocked it out? Christ, why couldn't she remember? But she admitted nothing and said even less, resealed the jiffy bag and asked, "Do you honestly think that only money buys new lives?"

It was the most decent thing Maggie Gifford could've done and Frank knew it. But he couldn't help himself. He put the envelope of cash back inside his jacket pocket then slat a two pound coin down on the table and told her it was for milk.

"I would've seen you, Maggie," he said slowly. "I can smell a drunk driver from ten miles away. I would've seen you. You wouldn't have hit me."

So that's why Frank had never shopped her.

"You were supposed to get the milk."

It was Jason. Hair stood on end and reeking of last night's stash, he picked up the two pound coin and looked at it for a very long time before he sat on his mother's thighs and taped it tight around her wrist with a thick black coarse tape that nicked her skin. Whilst he did, he said, "Every time you want a drink you hit yourself with that. Because if that's not a hammer to your head then I'm done. I'm out of fucking ideas with you." Then he rolled up his sleeves, watched her cower for a moment or two, turned his back on her, and started the washing up.

He chucked Frank a tea towel. "Get mucked in then, Frankie," he said grinning. "It's man's work is this."

They chewed the fat, Jason and Frank, about this, about that, and as best as they could. But that'd been twenty grand cash in an envelope. No-one in their right mind refused an envelope stuffed with twenty grand cash and no questions asked. As Frank wittered on, Jason realised that he'd have to sober his mother up if anyone was going to believe her, especially because he'd decided. Tomorrow, he would walk into a police station and demand a lot more cash than that.

Round 41

Lux said she was Constance's daughter. To her mind this was not a lie on her part, but a simple case of an overworked doctor partway through a double shift mishearing her. This would be her story. She might even shed a few tears when it came to retelling it. She had been there. She had watched her go. It was awful. It was a privilege. She was just so sorry that no-one else got there in time. She was surprised for how little she felt.

"Sometimes," said the registrar, "a fall can be like the flicking of a switch. It can kick start all that's being lying dormant."

"To off though," Lux had said. "It's a switch flicked off. Isn't that what you're saying?"

The registrar said that now maybe the time to call the family.

But Lux continued to sit and just stare. She knew she was the last person that Constance would want aside of her and she thought of the people she should call - Totty, Frank, the kids, even Malcolm - "But not me. You don't want me, do you Connie? He was never supposed to fall in love with me. And now you can't protect him from me anymore. But I can protect him from this."

She briefly thought of her children, twisting each thought so that she was right, she would be seen as doing right. She had rightly protected them from this too. She looked at Constance in the bed and then thought what an old child she seemed, milky white faced and smelling like sodden nappies. You are, she thought, just a child who likes to have all her own way.

And so she sat there. Someone else's daughter waiting for the last breaths of someone else's mother. Not even Constance's house could be here for her now.

"What's up Connie? Cat got your tongue?"

A little later and a little bored, Lux leant over Constance's body and began to rub away at the letters on the whiteboard above the bed that informed nurses, doctors, and visitors who'd never visited that she was Constance Minton. It didn't take long and, after she was done, Lux found herself smiling that the woman lying dying in the bed would now depart the world a **Con.**

"How fucking childish of me," she grinned at the bed.

*

After Constance died, Lux did try and call Totty again. Like she'd called three times from the hospital pay-phone last night with a fifty pence piece she'd cadged from a ward clerk. Her pay-as-you-go mobile was out of juice, her battery-charger still in the socket at home. *She had called.* Saturday night. Sunday morning. Not her fault Totty hadn't answered or that his phone suddenly went dead. She had tried. Tried his mobile. Tried the landline at Bennett Road. And she did think about going back into the ward to tell someone this but that wasn't her style. Once she'd made up her mind to walk the other way that's exactly what she did.

Round 42

It's the early 1990's. Before rave. After the strikes. Mid-way through Maggie's right to buy. Malcolm Gandy is twenty-five years old and courting houses. He has three on the go. He gives them girl's names. *Stacey. Charlotte. Alison.* He buys a fourth at auction for buttons. *Vanessa.* It takes him, with the help of Totty, a couple of months to get the lot spruced up and then he puts them up for rent for almost twice what the council had been charging. He realises, as he takes a young woman on a viewing around *Charlotte,* that he is missing another trick. This viewer is affluent, independent, and she doesn't want to live at home or rent from the council. "I'm better than that," had said this citizen rent. So the next two houses he buys - *Christina and Elizabeth* - he has split into two flats. A one-bed upstairs, a one-bed downstairs, shared bathroom, communal landing. He rents them both out to young women. Affluent. Independent. They become good pals. Drink wine at the weekends. Share problems. Date blokes. Until one falls pregnant and she moves out. The woman downstairs asks a friend to move in. Gandy says he has to charge her a bit more because he's had to redecorate.

Then Gandy gets a call. There's a row of terraces on Childwell Street and he can have them for a pound each. Gandy withdraws a ten pound note and shakes the hand of Councillor Roy Dingwall in the men's urinals in The Six Bells; a brown boozer by the bus station and known for its entertainment of the drunks and the dregs who can never be trusted to remember what they saw.

Gandy calls Frank. Wasn't your old dear's place No. 9 Childwell Street?

Frank watches from the bench in the park across the way as Gandy rolls in the bulldozers and jumps in the front seat himself to bring down No. 9. Police Constable Frank Blatch doesn't mind. Not now. He had minded though. And he'd fussed. Houses like that were bombproof. Surely, it was cheaper to do them up than knock them down and start again?

So Gandy had explained. Lead piping, he'd said, copper wires. Sockets in the skirting boards. Meter-boards held together by dust. No damp-proofing. No insulation. Single-glazed windows painted shut. Sewage pipe right outside the backdoor. Woodworm in the foundations. New building regulations coming in as Housing acts went out of fashion, all of it rewritten in the name of Health and Safety whilst the banks offered six, seven times your salary for a house you could never, in one lifetime, own. "Want me to carry on comrade?"

But they have a pact now, him and Malcolm, and what with him and Sissy trying for a baby. So he just watches as MG Estates throws up a block of a flats in a jiffy, bricks so paper-thin you could listen to the rows through the walls.

Constance minds. She minds very much. She reminds Gandy. "That was Ned's money Malcolm, and it wasn't given to you to profiteer. I need somewhere to live, you said. This is not what we agreed."

She was all about the guilt then. "You wouldn't even have one house if it wasn't for me, my money, my husband's life insurance, if me and Totty hadn't kept our traps shut over Jonty. It breaks my heart to know that Ned gave his life for you to start all this when this place is already dying. You're stigmatising council to make folk feel like being a private tenant sets them apart."

Gandy had agreed. "You're right Connie. Folk do feel stigmatised when stuck in council. I did, and you will be if you keep digging your heels in. Let me buy it for you."

Constance had covered her face with her hands. "I was like a mother to you, Malcolm Gandy."

"Yes," he'd said. "You were. But I never asked you to be so you've only got yourself to blame."

And she was to blame. She *is* to blame. She'd handed over Ned's meagre life insurance and kick-started the Gandy empire. Then here was the offer: have your pennies back Connie, or I'll buy your house for you.

"Which we'll rent off you."

"There'd be no rent."

"But you'd own it."

"Well, yes."

"So you're not buying it for me."

"Well, I am, until, well, you know."

"I die? And then what happens?"

"I have it back."

"And what about Totty?"

"He's a big boy Connie. If he hasn't sorted his shit out by the time you've gone then what hope do we have?"

"Yet you're brothers, Malcolm. You've been brothers all along."

"No we haven't Connie," Gandy had replied. "That's just something else you say when you want your own way."

He couldn't get through to her, she wouldn't listen, so he wrote her a cheque for £3,000 to replace the money he'd borrowed and she told him to never come into her house again.

But upstairs in his bedroom, Totty had heard it all. He had even overheard, "Frank can't give you what I can Connie, but it's a lot more than what your waste of space son could ever do, so if that's your choice, then that's your choice."

"I've not made *any* choice because I don't need to make a choice," Totty had heard his mother's quick retort.

"Well, it's my choice to leave you," had been Gandy's reply, so simple yet so very, very warning all the same.

Totty was thinking about this as he let himself in with the blunt end of a chisel tapped against a weak pane of glass in Frank's backdoor. He made himself at home. Filled the kettle. Hunted out teabags, a mug, let the bag steep whilst he took himself into the front room to sniff. Frank was flush, certainly, but that was a brand new settee still in its plastic body-bag.

Totty returned to the kitchen for his mug of tea. It was a different kettle. White. Plastic. He opened the fridge door. No milk. Frank never bought any milk. He took out the teabag with his fingers and headed for the bin. No bin either. He looked about him. Lifted the mug above his head to look underneath it. He didn't need to be able to read to know what Made in Taiwan looked like, but something wasn't right. He let the mug drop from his hand. Butterfingers. Now look what you've gone and done.

He scuffed at the kitchen wall with his work boot. Years ago, a dropped mug meant new business. Great men kept in their jobs. Now it just meant a trip to Tesco. No-one giving a shit for what they drank out of or for where it came from: how much it meant to family life. He kicked at the wall again. Then he kicked at it again, and then again, until he found he was running at it and booting it leaving skid-marks and boot-prints as if he'd been climbing up Frank's walls. He reached down for his tools and pulled out a spanner. A good one too. It'd been one of his best lifts from the hardware - old man Mole behind the till in his little handyman warren and no CCTV; so busy enquiring of his mother's health and reminiscing the old ways - Totty had been able to slip this into his pocket, slip that into his bag, and fill that toolbox to bursting.

He used the spanner first. It made a good dent in Frank's kitchen wall - the plaster beyond the paint had never hardened as it should - cheap stuff, botch job - and he pulled at the plasterboard, tearing away great chunks and kicking them about the kitchen floor. He'd never felt so alive. This was the sort of damage he'd been trying to cause all week and it felt good, really fucking good. He said out loud, "What I did doesn't come anywhere near to what I'm going to do."

Because Frank had seen Malcolm push Jonty Moffatt into the canal. He must've done. There was no way he couldn't have done. He'd been stood right next to him. Because shortly after Mr Hunt had stepped off his milk crate to step onto his wooden ladder to reach that jar of gobstoppers, Gandy had seen he was midway through a till count. Gandy's father always told him that they had all they needed. But Gandy wanted. And he wanted everything that was in that till. So they paid for the gobstoppers with what they'd cobbled together between them and Jonty Moffatt said "S'alright, I'll have the gum," just as Hunt's eyes drifted down south-west.

Totty can't quite remember what Hunt said. He knows he shouted. That he might've used the word stealing, certainly he'd shouted "Thief!" But Gandy was already yelling, "Run!" And so they did. The others had just thought it was a game - cops and robbers, pirates and bandits - but bloody bobbies on the beat in those days, they came out of nowhere, and they'd all carried on running down to the canal where perhaps they could dive into brambles; four mouths drooling, eight eyes streaming, and Totty, up ahead, had come to a sudden stop, swung around and shouted at Gandy, "Yer robbed him, didn't yer?" That's when they'd fallen into each other, when Gandy had looked behind him and seen the bobby gaining ground, still very much in pursuit. So Gandy had shouted again, "Run! Run for your lives!" And did so with his elbows so far out that there wasn't room for all of them on the bank.

What Totty can definitely remember is the sound of a body hitting water by mistake. And then he can remember comrade Blatch yelling, "Run all the way and don't stop 'til you get there." And so he did as he was told like any good boy should.

It could've happened anywhere. They could've been in any sweet shop, on any street in any town in any country in the world. *Run all the way and don't stop 'til you get there.* That brown dirty Trent and that grey stick of gum – "Fish me out! I can't swim! Fish me out!" Floor sweepings, potato peelings, rotten cabbages, and fish heads. He'd swallowed them all and grew heavy. And it could've happened anywhere. But it didn't. It was here. It'll all come out in the wash, they said. But Totty had just kept on running, looking for a father that didn't want to be found.

*

Totty took the stairs two at a time and pounded from one bedroom to another to another, because three bedrooms - Frank had three unused bedrooms - how did Frank get and Gandy so much and him nothing when they were all in this together? And Totty went at the three bedrooms with hammer and spanner, punching holes in the walls and stripping the wallpaper: he trashed each room, pulling out empty drawers, chucking them against the walls, destroying the silence, this semi-detached shrine, turning each room into a blast zone, and laughing as he did. It was frenzied but precise - *this is why we'd be better off without you* - and deep, in the pit of his stomach, the twisting kept on twisting, the churning kept on churning, the past kept on falling down around him, burying him alive.

Your life isn't as shit as you keep making out. You're just fucking bone idle.

It'd been a nasty stack of words to chuck together, they'd really punched hard, and they made every hair on the back of Totty's neck stand up. He thought of all the mugs slipping through fingers in England right now. Of women, on their hands and knees, with a dustpan and brush. He used to do that. That used to be him. When a mug slipped, a plate dropped, a cup came out misshapen and without its matching saucer. He swept up the odds, sods, and mish-mashes, the deformed and not-quite-perfect. Without him, the factory floor would've been a minefield of shattered crocks and porcelain shards, sharp as spears. No-one would've been able to walk through it without being cut. And that's why Totty Minton had been important. He'd kept the cogs clean. But it'd never bought him a single brick.

Then something out of Frank's bedroom window caught his eye; something with blue and more blue words. He looked closer, narrowing his eyes as if startled by sudden sun, and saw the sales-board nailed to the gatepost. He didn't need to be able to read to see what Frank had gone and done.

It's Another Gandy House & Home.

Ask Now About Renting Me!

Totty dropped to his knees. It was no longer Frank's house. What he'd trashed now belonged to Gandy. The bog-chain of his life had been well and truly pulled.

Round 43

The only way to protest is to occupy, thought Della, as she got into her car and began to drive. The only way to instigate change is to unite. At least Totty Minton was out there. At least he was doing something. Some of us, thought Della, need to have a go, for God, if nothing else, loves a trier. It took just one person to get a ball rolling, and she wanted to be able to tell her own daughter, her daughter's daughters: I did that. I was there. I did it for you.

And she was pissed off. That too.

Not because of Jake. He'd given her what she'd needed by showing her all he didn't want. And not because of her lack of maternity help. That was just bad luck. And failing to read the small print. No. It was because of everything she had never done. Apathy was the new malaise. Abstention just another way of copping out. By all means blame, but only if you can claim to have contributed, participated, tried. She was going to *do* something. She was going to stand by these poor people and help.

As she neared Bennett Road, however, she started to wish that she'd chosen a better outfit, something sharper, more purposeful, and not French plaited her hair like some old maid. She didn't look the part of a staunch campaigner, of someone going to make difference. All she had in her head was the word 'occupy' - *we will occupy Bennett Road* - and she spent a few minutes unravelling her hair from its plait and staring at the house through her windscreen, wondering what compelled the old dear to keep a window box full of so many synthetic flowers; why a crisp white net was so meaningful; when it was that these houses fell out of favour and the new-build took root; how the closing of the pot-banks had destroyed so much, taken all hope. Nothing works without workers, and it was because some of those workers were still going strong that fine bone china was still worth its weight in afternoon tea in, well, Dubai. Some traditions still burnt bright even if the chimneys didn't. But that didn't keep blokes like Totty Minton in work.

Her knocks on the Minton's front door were tentative, barely audible. If Totty answered, she was just going to say, "I know you're angry, but I'm listening," and then hope to God that he bought it. But no-one answered the door.

She had started down the passageway at the side of the house when it occurred to her that, actually, there was nothing to be done because there was too much to be done. History is only a beautiful creature to those who want to admire it, and life is far too busy to be bothering for what was when *what is* is so very crap. Besides, although she could see that there was nothing wrong with the house or even in the way that they lived, could she really take on Malcolm Gandy and bring him down brick by brick? After all, what he thought about the Mintons and Bennett Road had been said both loud and often enough now it was hard not to see that the area was a problem because *they* were the problem. If they'd just moved out, like everyone else had. And besides, Gandy, like all men who played the game well, would have answer after answer for every question she might throw his way until her head would spin so violently, she would throw up her hands and quit.

Nevertheless, she would tell her daughter one day that she had gone there with all good intentions and her heart in the right place, but like all her good intentions that were ruled by her heart, she'd just found herself feeling a bit daft and a lot taken in by a plight that perhaps wasn't a plight after all. Especially, if the gossip was to be believed; if Malcolm Gandy had actually offered them new houses for free. That was not to be sniffed at, and certainly not when a father. You provided a roof for your children no matter what.

So she hurried back down the passageway and towards her car, got back in, and drove away without anyone knowing she was even there.

Except Roy Dingwall had come for one last look before he made up his mind. And it was a great pity for him to have clocked Della from where he was parked on the other side of the street, because his mind had, at the time, still been erring on the side of hope. The street had once been kind to Roy and his mother, and it was a debt he felt he could perhaps payback by holding out for an overseas investor looking to bring the dead back to life and grow a few teapots again. But Della racing towards her car, she herself not long from giving birth, made him realise: everything comes to its natural end.

Roy was reaching into the glove compartment for his mobile phone when Jason Gifford rounded the corner with his hood up, an unlit cigarette sticking out of his mouth, his trousers heavy with chains, phones, and other gizmos he tended to filch as down payments. He coughed and spat and from this distance, he was, thought Roy, indicative of all that was wrong, all that was broken, why he'd switched allegiance and campaigned for a United Kingdom defined by discipline and rough justice, men with a business plan and other ideas up their sleeves, and he nearly jumped out of his skin when Jason knocked on his windscreen.

"Wanna buy some lighter fluid? I've got Valium, Xanax, make you real sociable, improve your life expectancy." Jason fished through his pockets. "These little fuckers' will have you eating your face off," he grinned through the windscreen waving a plastic bag full of little white pills. "What about this Zippo? You wanna buy this Zippo?" Jason was now offering up a lighter. "It's the fucking gold Rolex of Zippos is this. Twenty quid to you mate, my last offer."

It wasn't his Zippo. He was selling someone else's Zippo. That's how it was today. The only way to survive was to find something to sell.

"Come on," said Jason. "I know you want it. I know you've got money."

Roy flicked up the switch for the driver's window to snap shut and scrolled through the numbers on his mobile phone. "OK Malcolm," he said, not waiting for a greeting from the other end. "But this time I want in," and then he dropped his window and asked Jason how much it would cost for him to use that Zippo to torch that house over there. "Because I will Malcolm; I've got a kid with me right now who's ready to do it. I'll have the place torched if you dare undercut me again," and just like that, Bennett Road came to its natural end.

Round 44

Maggie Gifford was dressed in her husband's wedding suit with her make-up applied like egg stuck to a pan. She looked up at the steps in front of her and wished the bottle of water she carried was spiked. Instead, she rubbed at the two pound coin taped to her wrist and told herself *I don't want it, I don't need it*. Her son, seeing the movement in her hands, grabbed hold of her left and squeezed it gently. "Think," he whispered. "Think of me."

So she did. Like she always did. She walked into the police station with her head held high and her chest puffed out to inform the duty sergeant that she was here to report a few crimes.

It came out as a list: Harassment, alarm and distress, Section 5 of the Public Order Act for starters, attempted manslaughter - because he had stated, in no uncertain terms, that - "You can either put me out of my misery with this hammer to my head or you can choose solidarity and we can kick the fuck out of that wall" - which, to her mind, was him threatening her with terrible violence. And then only this morning she'd been blackmailed by an officer of the law to keep her mouth shut which had caused such a shitload of stress she was permanently shaking.

And yes, she could put a price on it, as she handed over to Derek Goodlove, her solicitor, who was going to negotiate the compensation claim on her behalf. "And tell them what's just happened this morning," Maggie nudged Jason. "Go on. Tell them what Roy Dingwall MP has just asked you to do."

Knockout

1   When does a house become your home?

a)   After six months   ☐

b)   When you say it out loud   ☐

c)   When you decorate   ☐

d)   When you put children in it   ☐

e)   Other   ☐

2   Why do some people drift from house to house?

a)   Transience and adventure   ☐

b)   Work   ☐

c)   Looking for roots   ☐

d)   To make money   ☐

e)   Other   ☐

3   What are people wanting when they say this doesn't feel like home?

a)   Stability, security   ☐

b)   Total ownership   ☐

c)   Decorated to their taste   ☐

d)   What their friend's house looks like   ☐

e)   Other   ☐

4   What does going home really mean?

a)   Somewhere where you can be yourself   ☐

b)   Where you're looked after   ☐

c)   Where you're meant to be   ☐

d)   Mum and Dad   ☐

e)   Other   ☐

"Why wasn't I born in Australia?" Kirty asks her brother, having found him squatting amongst the pirate camp on the living room floor of Fairview, and rooting through his father's holdall. She holds up her fingers. "Is it because (1) God wanted me to be born here so (2) I was meant to be here, or (3) Because dad saw mum on the bus and stopped mum going to Australia, or (4) Australia was full up and didn't need any more babies?"

Joss looks up at his sister still wearing granddad's glasses with the lenses pushed out, and now holding a clipboard as quiz master. He creases up his forehead as he pretends to think.

"Two," Joss says, with a click of his fingers. "Do I win a jet ski?"

"No," says Kirty. "You are the weakest link. Goodbye."

She comes and sits aside of her brother.

"Round nose," he goes.

"Big chin," she went.

"It's all about us," he says.

"Me and you," she says, and she puts her arms around his neck and looks down at the floor.

The contents of their two rucksacks have been emptied onto the bare floorboards: because Joss has been thinking about what they might eat, whether they should go looking for their dad, if they should just bed down for a second night, because this is their home now and he is the man of this house. He's also realised that his dad has not packed their school uniforms. He thinks:

Has he done that on purpose?

Are we not staying after all?

Or not going back to school?

Or did he need an excuse to go back to Bennett Road? To turn up on the doorstep and say - "Uniforms. Forgotten their uniforms" - and Constance would step aside and show him where they were hanging up, freshly ironed, and ready for Monday morning, their school shoes polished and shining and warming by the stove. And she would make tea. And perhaps toast. Hot chocolate for Kirty. And time would get on. And she'd say, "Well, you may as well stop here now." And they would. Because that's what they did. And wherever they were going to live would get forgotten because, as Constance would say in the morning, "This is your home, son. This is our home."

Kirty says - "We're not stopping here, are we?"

Joss looks at her and sees a little girl swindled. He says nothing and has one last pocket to look through before he tells her to pack up her rucksack: they are going home. He finds a Stoke City football sock fat with cash. He takes out the roll of notes and gawps at them, as if he's never seen money before.

Kirty gasps. "Has daddy robbed a bank?"

Joss rubs at his face. Runs a hand through his hair. Flicks through the roll of notes and makes a wild guess - two, no, more like three thousand pounds, there has to be - he's running away. His father is going to run away, if he hasn't already gone, in which case, is the money for them? And then Kirty whoops - blue flashing lights are streaking down the road and that means only one thing.

"Uncle Frank!" she shouts, and runs to the door.

Because Totty Minton has been found by a resigned Frank Blatch curled up like a dying dog on a hearth rug. He's been formally charged with affray, damage to public property, and breaking and entering with intent, before Frank has checked his comrade's pulse for life.

"I could go on, Totty," he'd said, feeling about Totty's left wrist which he'd gouged into with a loose screw from one of Frank's kitchen cupboards. "I know you hear me. You do know what is happening?"

"But my name is Josiah," Totty had whispered up at Frank. "As in Wedgewood, as in Spode, as in man and his brother."

Frank had told him to hush - don't be wasting your breath on all your daft shit now lad - and he'd tied his handkerchief about Totty's wrist to stop the bleeding.

Totty's eyes had flickered as Frank had confiscated his father's claw hammer and dropped it into a plastic bag as if it were a murder weapon to be reckoned with. Then Frank had taken a pair of pliers to Totty's leash and the weight had dropped away. He'd felt as light as a feather, like a leaf swinging from a tree, and he was scooped up like a little boy and carried out into the afternoon lull. Then, Frank had whispered into sunbeams that, "Connie's gone comrade, she's gone, so you hold on, you hold the fuck on for those kids."

And as he'd continued to whisper the stories of how it was going to be - three bedrooms comrade, a bay window, enough of a garden to stretch your legs - the screw behind Ned's photograph came loose. It slipped off the kitchen wall and dropped right behind the stove, and because no-one else ever lived at 13 Bennett Road, it stayed where it was all forgotten, until Gandy's bulldozers rolled in and it just became part of the rubble.

Thank you

To Phil Breeze, Becky Henderson, Deb Jones, Ami Price, Len & Jim Carpenter, Jack & David, Jon Crew, Kate Halls, Mags & Steve Fenwick, Maz Reader, Petra Boddington, Emma Stuart, Lucio Buffone, Louisa Clews, Ernie Opuni, Laura & Lee Roberts, Jo & Dan North, Lord & Lady Moncrieff, Rachel Jennings, Siani Hughes, Huw Davies, Nick Button, Laura Creyke, the original Fat Boy - Liam Carty, and the best man & the best woman ever, John and Sandra Lane - For a lorra love and listening, always.

To Ian Davidson and Helen Wilcox for your never-ending guidance, patience and advice; to Dr Nicola Wilson and Dr Catherine Burgass whose support and collaboration has been both grateful and inspiring; to all at Writing West Midlands and every brilliant writer I've been lucky enough to know on Room 204.

Huge thanks to the incredible talents that are Luke Wright, Niall Griffiths, and Stuart Maconie, for taking the time to read and support this book.

To the tour de force that is Anna Dreda and her sterling Wenlock Books team.

Unwavering thanks to Philippa Brewster for sticking by me through thick, thin, and many versions; to Rachael Kerr for believing in me and this novel; to Tania Harrison for being ruddy marvellous; to Paul McVeigh and Cathy Galvin for giving me a chance; to Nadia Kingsley for making a dream come true.

To my family who enable every word I write and encourage me wholeheartedly to write more. I couldn't do it without any of you.

And to Dave, because I don't know how you do it and I'm forever in awe how you do.

This book is also in the memory of the glorious Eric Welsh. *Writing is my holy land, pet.*

About the Author

Born in Stoke-on-Trent, Lisa Blower won the Guardian Short Story Competition in 2009, was shortlisted for the BBC Short Story Award in 2013, and Highly Commended in the 2015 Bridport Prize. Her short fiction has appeared on Radio 4, in Comma Press, the Luminary, the New Welsh Review, and Literary Salmon. She is a lecturer in Creative Writing and the 2016 Writer in Residence at Shrewsbury Museum and Art Gallery. *Sitting Ducks* is her first novel.

www.lisablower.com